Unthaw My Heart

Harmony Noble

TrueLoveWriters

Revised Edition: March 29, 2026

ISBN 978-1-963074-61-1 & ISBN 978-1-963074-00-0

Story creation, cover, and illustrations by Melody Noble & Harmony Curtis

Thank you for choosing this book.
We hope the story
brought you as much joy reading it
as we had in creating it!

We'd love to hear from you! Feel free to reach out via email at TrueLoveWriters@gmail.com, and follow us on Instagram, Facebook, TikTok at @truelovewriters for the latest updates and behind-the-scenes fun.

Get access to exclusive offers, bonus content, new release updates, and recommendations for more great reads.

Sign up for our e-newsletter at HarmonyNoble.com.

This book is dedicated to the **incredible strength** and **beauty** of trans and queer individuals who understand **love knows no bounds**, to those who have faced adversity with **unwavering courage**, and to those who continue to **champion love** in all forms.

You are not just accepted— *You are cherished, celebrated, and loved.*
Your presence and your love enriches the world, and this story is a small tribute to your resilience and the power of love.

YOU ARE WORTHY, ALWAYS AND FOREVER.

Unthaw My Heart

Harmony Noble

TrueLoveWriters

Prologue: Makayla Jackson

One Year Ago, Christmas Eve in Anchorage, Alaska

Despite the festive gold decorations and soft Christmas carols piped in, the fluorescent lights harshly illuminated the worried families and exhausted staff in the hospital cafeteria. The clatter of trays and loud floor polisher drown out the sound of my heart pounding with trepidation.

Bryant, my coworker, and boyfriend, stands before me. His voice—smooth as velvet but laced with male confidence—carries across the cafeteria. The calculated words command not just mine but everyone's attention.

His blue eyes sparkle with charm as he towers over me and announces, as if on a mountain and not in the sleepy cafeteria, "*Doctor* Makayla, *my love*, I can no longer keep this secret locked away within me. Will you do me the honor of becoming my wife? Will you marry me and make me the happiest man in the world?"

God, give me strength! I must be dreaming because Bryant and I have only dated for a few months, and honestly, this is unexpected.

In an instant, Bryant is kneeling, the master orchestrator of a grand performance, and he produces a box from his pocket, opening and revealing my mother's diamond ring.

"What?" I brush my greasy hair from my face, blinking hard. *Did he talk to my parents, and they consented, giving him the ring to propose?* I guess it makes sense. My mom loves him, as he attends Mass with us at St Mary's Catholic Church, and his parents also attended St Mary's school. Plus, she wants grandchildren like *yesterday.*

The atmosphere is charged with expectation as eyes move from Bryant to the ring and me. The crowd holds its breath, waiting for my response.

This cannot be real! Perhaps I fell asleep during my night shift, and I'm dreaming. The only reasonable explanation is that my head rests on a keyboard at the Emergency Room nurses' station.

But I see my new friend Jessica, who's orienting me to the Emergency Department. Marianne, my mom's childhood friend, the hospital administrator who hired me, is waiting, along with the other staff, watching me, the *new* doctor. The spectacle of their friend, a handsome man, proposing to a tired doctor in front of everyone on Christmas Eve is *too cheesy* to be in my dreams.

I'm awake, and everyone is waiting for my response.

The question fills the air, suffocating me. My heart races, and for a fleeting moment, I think of running.

Jessica smiles and nudges me.

Who wouldn't want to marry the popular and respected Respiratory Therapist, Bryant?

I glimpse my reflection in the napkin holder—my brown eyes red and puffy from the long shift. Despite the vice squeezing my chest, I put on my doctor's confident smile.

He hands me a tissue, thinking I'm overwhelmed and these are happy tears. Then he pulls me closer, his grip firm, and says, "Looks like a *YES.* We're engaged, and you're all invited to the wedding!"

The crowd claps, their eyes filled with envy and admiration, believing this is the pinnacle of a fairy tale romance - a handsome man proposing to a beautiful woman in an unlikely place.

My thoughts whirl, and my heart is in my throat. *Say No!*

He kisses me lightly, his lips branding me, marking his territory, as everyone claps and begins congratulating him. The people in the cafeteria titter and giggle with excitement.

I didn't say yes!

I reach toward him, and he takes the offered hand, slipping on my family ring. My mouth is too dry to talk, and my eyes dart around the room. "Bryant, this. . . caught me off guard. . .," I say.

He leans closer. "Mak Attack, you are perfect for me: ravishing, a doctor, rich, and Catholic. And I'm perfect for you. We'll be the hospital's power couple. You won't disappoint me, our friends, and your family." He winks at me and smiles broadly at the crowd.

I hate the nickname Mak Attack!

I'm exhausted from my shift, and I *do like* Bryant. Obviously, I've considered marriage, or I wouldn't be dating him. I've spent the bulk of my twenties training and schooling to land my dream job, working as an Emergency Room Psychiatrist. My next goal is to have a big family. And an engagement is *just dating* with the promise of marriage, after all.

I want this, right?

"Amazing, Dr. Mak," Nurse Jessica says, pulling me away from Bryant for a hug. "You're on fire. Snagging this ER job and now snagging the most eligible bachelor. What's your secret?"

Prologue: Pauline Jacobs

One Year Ago, Christmas Eve in Syria's US Army Camp

A blaring siren shatters the night's stillness, slicing through the fabric of darkness like a jagged blade. I wake with adrenaline coursing through my veins, a surge of raw fear. My surroundings are disorienting for a heartbeat—scratchy wool, dusty air, and the heavy humidity crushing me.

It's the desert—the unforgiving, fucking desert, where the Army posted me.

A heavy foreboding settles in the pit of my stomach, a dreadful hunch. My fingers tremble, lacing my combat boots. The familiar ritual usually grounds me, but it intensifies my jumpiness today.

My gut tells me *something's wrong.* I rush into the heart of the bustling machine shop; the tang of grease and the chorus of clattering tools embrace me like old friends. *There's nothing wrong-my gut lied.*

Officer Curtis spots me. "Hey, Jacobs! Coming in early?"

My gaze dances across the faces of my comrades, each one working and ignoring the near-constant sirens. Amidst the clinking tools and jokes, these men are my family in this unforgiving place—a family forged by shared work and an unspoken understanding. I finally found a place where I fit. I am not *a woman, a lesbian, a gearhead,* or *a small-town freak.* I'm a soldier.

I nod at Curtis and the mundane scene of my platoon working on engines with the hum of holiday music from the radio. "Had a gut feeling something was up. But it's probably Johnson fuckin' around with my tools—"

Then, in the blink of an eye, an explosion shatters the shop, sending shockwaves and metal crashing upon us. The once-familiar garage transforms into a nightmare of twisted metal and agonizing cries. Smoke and debris blur my vision, a suffocating haze amplifying the pain shooting through my body as I lie on the floor. A thousand needles prick my skin, and my vision turns black, telling me to close my eyes and surrender.

Chapter 1

Mak

SNOW CHAINS REQUIRED.

My attention snaps from the mesmerizing white landscape to the road sign illuminated by my Jeep's headlights.

The powdery snow flits lazily across my windshield, a whirling dance, as my tires carve a deep path through the snow-covered road. On Christmas Eve, the daylight is fading early at four in the afternoon. The tranquil, remote Caribou Hills is silent and frosty.

Buzz. Buzz. Buzz.

I glance at my phone in my cup holder, trying to get my attention with the glowing, vibrating ringing. It's another call from Bryant, my ex-fiancé, trying to convince me not to go to the cabin alone. But as soon as my eyes dart back to the road, they widen, my muscles tense, and my hands squeeze the steering wheel as I crest an icy slope. The tires lose their grip, floating over the road, and my knuckles turn white, clenching the steering wheel that no longer controls my Jeep.

"No! No! Not now!" I cry futilely. My stomach moves to my throat, suffocating me, and my left hand reflexively moves to cover the Saint Michael's medallion at my throat.

My car is in an icy, downhill freefall, and I can't stop it as I careen down the steep slope. My breathing shallow, I yank the steering wheel following the direction of the slide, praying for traction. Miraculously, the tires catch before I enter the deep ditch, allowing me to wrestle back control from the icy road.

I mutter a prayer of thanks, but the tires skate again, not responding to my direction. I desperately try to steer back onto the road, but the laws of physics are working against me. In a cruel twist of fate, the Jeep gains speed, skating faster down the hill as if it's building up momentum for a triple axel instead of slowing for the corner.

"Oh God!"

In sheer panic, my foot slams down the brake pedal, my final attempt to regain control and stop the slide. Instead, the Jeep gives me a bone-jarring jolt, veering off the road and the snowy ditch, unable to stop its speed as it *whooshes* and *thumps,* making me squeeze my eyes shut.

Being unable to stop my Jeep from throwing me into the surrounding dark woods is worse than nicking an artery during surgery—at least an artery can be clamped and repaired. I'm powerless to the disorderly elements, and I'm without my hospital team to help.

Thump.

My breath hitches as the Jeep suddenly stops, jerking my body forward. I open my eyes to the blurry snow and darkness outside my windshield. My hands remain locked on the wheel as adrenaline shoots through me like an electric shock—my heart pounds. My lungs ache for air. My hands are clenched and shaking from my close call.

The adrenaline hits my brain, allowing me to process the situation and shift into my emergency room autopilot.

Gingerly peeling my fingers from the steering wheel, one by one, I check that each of my digits is functional. I'm uninjured but can't stay in the Jeep, as no one will see me this far off the road. I look at my phone- *no signal* and my gaze drifts upward, landing on the road thirty feet away. My stomach churns as my brain processes the harsh reality. Between the deep snow and the distance uphill, there's no way my Jeep is getting back to the road.

And who knows when anyone else will be driving down this remote road. I don't have any snow gear, food, or water because I dropped everything off at the cabin days ago for my annual Christmas Eve holiday. This is my first year without my parents, and I plan to enjoy a quiet, cozy holiday-just me with a sweet romance novel and hot chocolate in front of the fire.

My cabin isn't too far, and the snow is increasing. I must leave immediately before whiteout conditions hit, or navigating there will be impossible.

I'm hiking through the snow to the cabin.

I change the gear into park, and the engine's low hum is the only sound in the eerie stillness. Shaking, I turn off the Jeep, cutting off the engine noise.

"Dear Lord, give me strength," I whisper, tucking my holiday hat over my head and zipping up my woefully thin jacket.

Opening the door, the wind and icy snow slap my face, and I tug the Santa hat further down as my boots crunch against the unforgiving ice, a bleak soundtrack to the frozen challenge of walking back to the road and then to my cabin.

Teeth chattering, I trudge onward, a lone figure walking in the biting cold. Every breath creates an icy halo around me. Trying to stay calm, I wrap my arms around my shivering body, attempting to preserve my heat. My fingers are frozen sausages, aching with the cold, and only the garish Santa cap shields me from the biting wind.

I berate myself for this unlucky situation. *Why? Why didn't I take the time to ensure I had my winter chains in my Jeep?*

The thought of an Alaskan Emergency Room doctor freezing to death on Christmas Eve in a blizzard is absurd—*Impossible!* And someone discovering me on Christmas, frozen solid in my cheesy Santa hat, makes me want to throw the hat into the woods. But I like my ears, and frostbite is no joke.

My plan was to be nestled warm in my cabin for the holiday, far from the chaos of work and the fresh wounds of my recent breakup with Bryant. Instead, I'm slogging through knee-deep snow, battling an unexpected Alaskan blizzard.

"Time to check for a signal," I mutter aloud. The sound of my voice solidifies my resolve as I trudge onward.

And there *it* is, the last message from Bryant lighting up my phone screen. *Call me if you need anything. I'll come out there and join you, Mak Attack.*

The words hang in the air, my mind playing them on a loop, and I yell at the useless *phone, him, the blizzard.* "I'm *stranded.* No one can find me! Bryant, I wouldn't call you *if* I had cell reception. *I DON'T LOVE YOU!"*

The snow muffles the words as it obscures the moon and starlight. My cheeks flush with embarrassment as I replay the disappointment clouding Bryant's face when I ended our engagement weeks ago and his desperate attempts to convince me that "love grows from friendship" and I needed to "give *us* more time."

However, the truth is, *my heart is telling me Bryant isn't the one.* Freezing to death is karma's way of punishing me for shattering a man's heart who did nothing wrong but love the wrong woman.

With each freezing step into the wind, I'm kicking myself for my poor clothing choice. Jeans were an unfortunate decision, and my feet should be warm in wool socks, not my thin cotton work socks. The Alaskan winter is unforgiving and doesn't care about my cold feet and misery.

Adding to my regrets, I didn't check that my snow chains were in the Jeep when I rushed out of the house. And confounding my misfortune, I didn't stop at the Ninilchik gas station to put on the chains before going off-road. If I had, I would have realized I didn't have them and bought another pair to put on the Jeep. The gas station attendant might even have warned me about the weather, and I wouldn't be in this predicament.

No one but Bryant, hours away in Anchorage, even knows I'm out here.

I clap my hands together to get the blood flowing.

Why did I bolt without snow gear and chains? I'm Alaskan AND a doctor—I should know better!

In any other place, calling Roadside Assistance would be a no-brainer. But here, miles from civilization, with no cell service and zero chance of a tow truck locating me. I'm an idiot for not using snow chains and my stupid clothing choice.

Still, I bite my dry bottom lip and tightly smile to maintain my optimism. *At least I'm able to walk rather than being crushed inside my crashed Jeep.* In Alaska, danger lurks in every pristine snowdrift, as I know from working in Emergency Medicine.

I'm alive, walking, and I will make it to my cabin.

The wind howls around me, cutting through my clothing.

Why didn't I pack my snow gear? Why didn't I bring a thermos of hot chocolate?

My thoughts spiral negatively, but the thoughts distract me from an even bleaker possibility—succumbing to hypothermia and dying alone in this relentless snowstorm.

And why don't I love my handsome fiancé, Bryant? That's the million-dollar question I ask myself too many times and can't seem to answer.

He cares about me and wants me to spend the holidays with him, not at the cabin. And if I'd have shown him any kindness and asked before rushing out of the house, he would've put the snow chains on the Jeep.

The scene, hours old, plays out in my mind. Coming home from work, I planned to shower and dress, then head to my parents' cabin. But Bryant was home, lingering, trying to talk me out of going, to instead stay home with him and make a new holiday tradition.

I don't need a new tradition! Also, I'm not marrying him, so he will *not* be part of my upcoming holiday traditions.

He hasn't moved out, and he's not accepting the break-up well despite me bluntly sharing my feelings with him.

We haven't officially announced our breakup to our coworkers. So, on top of being exhausted from a shift at the hospital, where all my coworkers wished me a Merry Christmas with my new fiancé, I have to find the energy to tell him, *again,* that I'm not *marrying him* and forcefully eject him from our home.

Our hospital schedules are chaotic at St Mary's Alaska Medical Center, where we work, and this cabin trip was supposed to give me some much-needed space and time to reflect. But Bryant ignored my plans.

He lit candles and baked Shepherd's Pie when I arrived home. I had hoped he'd pack his things and move out before Christmas, but he's attempting to rekindle our nonexistent love.

His voice echoes, "Mak, can't you see I'm perfect for you? We're getting married, and we work together. Your parents approved of us! You are ruining a perfect relationship. What will everyone think when you tell them you're dumping me?"

I didn't argue—I fled my house and Bryant's dinner for the cabin. I have everything I need at the Caribou Hills cabin. Moreover, *I need to be alone.*

That was my first mistake!

Why did I let his arguments bother me? Why can't I get him to accept we are no longer together, and he'd be better off with anyone but me? I cannot marry someone I don't love!

Since my parents' funeral, we haven't been happy. *Really, we weren't jolly before, either.* Their sudden death made me reevaluate my life and my happiness. Instead of clinging to Bryant for support, I found myself pushing him away, realizing that just because he is perfect on paper, attending the same church, working with me, having similar hobbies, and having my parents' approval, it didn't mean he was the right person for me.

If he's my soulmate, why am I so unhappy when we are together?

Our interactions are tense and resentful, with him trying too hard to be friendly and irritating me. It's a cycle of dating, fighting, apologizing, and dating again. We are functional at work, in the chaos of the Emergency Room. But, our relationship crumbles outside St Mary's, and we aren't even friendly roommates anymore, giving each other the silent treatment, driving separately to work, and sleeping in different rooms.

To be fair, we've *always* slept in separate rooms because of our Catholic values. And perhaps that's why Bryant is rushing our engagement. It's hard for a modern guy to wait almost a year before sex, even if he is Catholic.

"Arrrrgh!" I yell into the night.

Unable to feel my extremities, I curse my decision to run away to the cabin.

Why did I trust the Jeep would safely make this sixty-mile journey through the Alaskan wilderness? Last week the trip was easy.

There are no signs of life, no roadway markers, an endless expanse of snow-covered tundra far removed from the Alaskan highway system, and no cell towers out here. The cabin is even more remote, miles away from the dirt road.

If my rough calculations hold, I'm a mere two miles away. I *must* summon the strength to hike there.

I shut my eyes briefly, attempting to revive my frozen eyeballs, but darkness offers no respite. Despite my horrible situation, I'm not hypothermic—no confusion, hallucinations, or slurred speech.

I can make it. I WILL make it to the cabin!

At the cabin, I have my winter gear and a ready wood stove. But the looming question is, *what if I don't make it?*

My shaking body and my fast, shallow breaths urge me to hurry. *Dying is not an option!*

How can I be in this situation?

I should *be happy* in my *perfect* relationship with my new job, having a cozy holiday with my family—*not freezing to death alone in the dark tundra!*

Chapter 2

Paul

The cool concrete floor on my face brings me back to reality. I look up at the people surrounding me and murmuring around me.

"Paul, Paul." My mother breaks through the haze and people, snapping me back to the present. I remember a distant boom, but everything from then until now is a blur.

"Mom, uh." I clear my throat, attempting to regain my composure. "Sorry," I mumble to the crowd and get onto my feet.

The booming fireworks must have triggered me. My heart jackhammers as if the enemy is bombing my army bunker. Beads of sweat coat my brow, and I attempt to regain control over my racing heart with the slow, measured breaths I've practiced at therapy.

My mother, always understanding, steps in, diverting their attention. "Paul's okay. He just needs some air. How about some of my famous rummy eggnog, everyone?"

The crowd obediently disperses, drawn to the promise of warm eggnog. My mom's a pro at handling situations like these. She touches the pin on her lapel; those blue, pink, white, pink, and blue stripes symbolize her support and understanding. She's been with me through my struggles with defining my identity and living with PTSD.

My dad, ever the military man, engages our neighbors in cheerful conversation, a deliberate distraction from his kid's breakdown. He might not express it openly, but his silent support speaks volumes.

I close my eyes and take deep breaths, focusing on the mantra my VA therapist instilled in me. *Breathe in*—one hour at a time, one day at a time. *Breathe out*—let the tension flow away. *There's no enemy here, no threat, just war's residue.*

"Why is your daughter a guy now?"

A child's innocent curiosity pierces through my racing thoughts, and I grimace as I pull myself up.

She's only asking what everyone is thinking.

My mom kneels to the child's level and explains, "Oh, sweetie, Paul is like a superhero who's about to put on his cape to become the hero he truly is. You know how superheroes have secret identities and don't show their true selves at first? A trans man is like that. Paul's a superhero who knows deep inside that he's a boy, even though he was assigned a different gender at birth. Superheroes know, but the world doesn't always recognize them."

The child nods. "Like Wonder Woman."

My mom smiles as the pigtailed girl skips off for another sugar cookie.

I take a deep breath, my racing heart now steadying. My momentary breakdown and my mom's impromptu explanation leave a bitter taste in my mouth.

"I'll haul the sled over to the Taylor's with the propane," I grumble, with my need for solitude and an escape from the party spurring me into action. The garage calls, a haven where I can lose myself in the familiar hum of diesel engines and assist my parents in their propane fuel delivery business.

Getting away from the curious looks and ceaseless chatter is non-negotiable.

The snowmobile carries me through a blur of snow-covered trees, their forms rushing past like white streaks. Delivering propane to a customer's remote cabin miles outside Ninilchik relaxes me.

My parents gave me this job delivering fuel and fixing diesel engines in Pop's shop. They worry, fully aware of the grim statistics concerning returning soldiers and their battles with mental health, and keep me close to watch over me.

They are right to worry.

My return to civilian life here in my hometown is one hell of a challenge. Dealing with my PTSD, a relentless burden, is made worse by what my VA therapist labels as survivor's guilt. *I'm a shit show!*

Before my military service, I didn't fit the mold, even of a tomboy. Tall and gangly, I defy societal expectations, especially in small-town Alaska. Sports held no appeal for me, and I had no interest in the boys who pursued me.

Instead, I sought solace in my mechanical pursuits, tinkering with greasy engines while other girls in my class focused on fashion and dolls. When I graduated, the military became my refuge, where gender distinctions didn't matter. Skill and determination were the only yardsticks.

Glancing down at my wrist, I glimpse ink peeking from beneath my glove—a heavy black army insignia with an unmistakable wrench and rifle. My teeth work to pull the glove back, covering it while my other hand instinctively tightens into a fist over the handlebars.

In the army, I was the only woman in our diesel shop, but I was a vital cog in a well-oiled machine.

Fast forward six months, and the Army bid me an early farewell, thanks to my cursed post-concussion migraines and dizziness. Fixing tanks and Jeeps became an impossible task. The doctors labeled the malingering symptoms as PTSD, a shitty gift from my time in the warzone. Discharged and adrift back home, I attempted the four-hour drive to the Anchorage VA hospital for the prescribed treatment regimen. But even in my quiet childhood home, sleep remains elusive, and I cancel more therapy appointments than I attend, retreating, haunted by the relentless memories of men, sirens, and explosions.

My roots run deep in Ninilchik, where I grew up in a small village community. Despite being a *local,* the villagers treat me like an outsider, avoiding me and calling me the "Dyke on the Bike," as if homosexuality is contagious.

I let their words slide, busy with my mechanical hobbies. In a town with limited options, I found my niche: trucks. I'm the best diesel mechanic these folks have seen. Fortunately, fixing engines and my parents' propane deliveries don't demand much human interaction, which suits me.

My parents, bless their hearts, have a mantra: "We don't live in Alaska to be city folks. We are villagers, part of a community where everyone knows everyone. We might not have city amenities, but we have the *real small-town Alaska.*" But living remotely also means access to regular therapy and medical care is as elusive as restful sleep for me.

Yet, here I am, instead of accepting my parents' care and the VA's help, I'm taking reckless chances riding into a snowstorm, testing the thin ice on streams, and pondering a question that shouldn't cross my mind: *If I were to vanish tonight, would it cast a permanent shadow over my parents' Christmas Eve? Wouldn't it be easier not to go home?*

The howling wind and relentless snow bring to mind the Alaskan elders' tales, those who, in their ailing years, chose to wander into the wilderness, leaving behind their tribes, burdens, and worries. Theirs is an honored departure, giving more food and resources to the rest of the tribe.

A desperate thought flickers through my mind—*it'd be easier to disappear into these unforgiving landscapes, to let the cold and isolation claim me, sparing my loved ones the constant struggle of supporting my broken soul.* The idea is a shadow, but it lingers.

As I zip through the snow-covered trail, my trained eyes automatically scan the surroundings. Something strange catches my attention—a distant figure, an anomaly in the snowy landscape.

Instinctively, my training kicks in, and I tense up before reminding myself to breathe.

Stay calm.

It must be a lone moose meandering along the dark trail or a caribou seeking refuge from the cold in the shallow snow rather than the deep snow in the ditches. After all, dusk has settled, and the wildlife follows the most accessible paths navigating this tundra.

Drawing closer, it's not a moose. The figure moves, unsteady and faltering—*It's a person!*

The diminutive person is in dark pants, a lightweight jacket, and, *unbelievably,* a festive Santa hat sparkling from the headlight. The figure sways erratically, veering toward the side of the trail before collapsing. My heart clenches in my chest as I realize the gravity of the situation: *a person walking at night in a blizzard with no one around but me.*

Shit!

My instincts kick into high gear as I approach and stop next to the dark form in the snow, invisible if I didn't know where to look. I yell over the engine's roar to check if they're conscious. But there's no movement in the dark lump.

The figure stirs, their activity a strange mix of stiffness and floppiness as if their body can't decide how to function. Slowly, they manage to push themselves up and shuffle towards me.

"Hold on," I call out, my words snatched away by the relentless wind. I stride over with my long legs and lift the limp form into my arms.

"Let me help you," I repeat, but my voice disappears into the frigid night.

I carry the person to my snowmobile, my well-worked hard muscles and height easily allowing me to lift the smaller, rounder person. I settle them awkwardly on the bench seat.

It's a young woman out here alone, in the middle of nowhere, dressed in gear hardly suitable for this kind of weather. Questions swirl in my mind, demanding answers, but the priority is clear: *Get her to safety and warmth before this blizzard kicks into high gear.*

She clings to me as I assist her, wrapping both arms tightly around my frame. My cheeks flame and adrenaline surges through me because I haven't felt the arms of another person in too long to remember.

"What are you doing out here? Where's your snowmobile?" I ask, my tone clipped and to the point.

"My Jeep ... it crashed on the corner of Falls Creek. I wasn't sure if I'd make it ..." she says, thankfully opening her eyes as she sputters through her chattering teeth. Her voice wanes, tears build in her eyes, and she slumps against me out of energy.

I give her a slight shake to wake her, and she points westward, which I hope indicates her cabin is nearby. *She could be pointing to the building storm, though.*

I need to get her to shelter, and I'm already twenty miles away from Ninilichik.

Her cabin is the best option.

I make another attempt to get answers. "You're out here alone. Where's your cabin?"

She points again. "Just past the stream ... the one with the orange door."

I know the odd orange-doored cabin, although it's not on my delivery list. It's not far from here.

Good! It must have a wood stove and, hopefully, people there to help.

They better have dry wood and hot coffee at her cabin. With this raging storm, there'll be power outages, and we'd be lucky if there's a phone line intact with the wind gusts attacking and knocking down the creaking trees surrounding us.

"I'll take you to your cabin and get you warmed up. Then we can figure out what to do about your Jeep," I outline. My military-sharp mind formulates a plan. I know what's required to save her life, and I intend to do it.

All my army medic training comes rushing back. Losing body heat and exposure to the cold is fatal, and the quickest remedy is to share your body heat with your comrade. I envelop her within my frame, tucking her body in front while reaching around her to hold onto the snowmobile, my eyes inexplicably glistening with moisture. I settled in behind her. My arms wrap around her to provide comfort and support.

I feel her relaxing into my embrace. Her shimmering eyes lock onto mine as tears begin to flow. My instincts make me tighten my hold as I offer her warmth and support.

It's been *forever* since I've touched another person. As I sit behind her, holding her close, my body slowly softens—a tingling sensation courses through my veins, unfamiliar and electric. I've not felt a connection with another person since working alongside my platoon.

As we speed toward her cabin, I sneak glances at her, studying her soft, full features and lustrous black hair. My heart beats with a different rhythm, and I realize this is a chance to make a difference. Amid the improbable snowy wilderness, I find this beautiful Latino woman, and my unique skills are needed to save her.

The heaviness and kicking in my chest are unexpected and unfamiliar feelings. Amid my plans to lose myself *alone* in this storm, I found a connection—*a purpose.*

The snowmobile hums beneath us as we navigate this *damn* relentless storm, each twist and turn to bring us closer to her cabin.

As the cabin comes into view, its orange door a beacon against the white backdrop, a wave of relief washes over me.

We've made it!

The tension in her body eases, and she leans further into me, her relief palpable at arriving at the cabin.

I guide the snowmobile to a gentle stop before the cabin, the engine's growl subsiding into a hushed silence. As I help my frozen passenger off the seat, her eyes are closed, and her body is unmoving.

My nerves fire, and my breathing increases. I look around. The cabin is dark and uninhabited. There's no help here or for miles.

I need to work faster!

Chapter 3

Mak

My heart races, a wild drumbeat against the backdrop of the blizzard's fury, each snowflake emphasizing my desperate situation. However, God has an odd sense of humor, and as I'm contemplating a future as an Alaskan popsicle, a rescuer on a snowmobile appears from the icy darkness of the storm.

Thank God! Someone is here!

I squint through the blinding snow. My rescuer is a genuine Christmas Eve miracle. Tears fill my eyes, and I put my hand on my neck, covering my medallion. *God answered my prayers in the nick of time.*

I pause and swallow. *My rescuer better not be a hypothermic hallucination!*

I hear his shouting.

He's real!

I numbly follow his lead, unable to talk or move. He places me in front to hold the handlebars as he wraps my frozen body with his sturdy frame, and an immediate rush of warmth flushes me. My relief floods me as I lean my icy body back into the stranger's sturdy frame. My eyes brim with a wordless thanks as we ride.

His unexpected, strong, extra-tight embrace on the snowmobile brings me more warmth.

I'm saved from this freezing nightmare and dropped into a dramatic rescue movie. Our connection is fiery hot, and even as my teeth chatter, I imagine this as a sweet Hallmark movie and not the popular brooding, anti-romance novels my friend Jessica reads at work.

As his arms envelop me, I'm powerless with the strength in them and his protectiveness. It's more than cold, making me tremble. There's something about this stranger who's come to my rescue, sending shivers down my spine and making me fantasize about romances.

The montage plays out in my numb mind with us reaching the cabin, having a playful snowball fight, rolling in the snow together, and then laughing over a cup of hot chocolate to the swelling of a soft, romantic ballad strumming. The scene's end would be me leaning into the handsome rescuer and our lips meeting sweetly, cozy in front of the wood fire.

I'm shielded from the biting wind inside his muscular frame as we race through the snow-covered trails to my cabin, and he revives my spirit and confidence.

I'm safe!

The snowmobile's growl harmonizes with the noise of my heart roaring in my ears. With each bump, twist, and jolt, I cling to him, my lifebuoy in the raging sea. My rescuer's attentiveness and protective presence draw me closer—his warmth seeping into my very bones, melting away the numbness.

Amidst my gratitude and borderline hypothermia, my mind clears. Despite the catastrophe and my near-death, one truth is undeniable—I'm ready to let go of Bryant and our toxic relationship *for good.*

God put me in this situation for a reason, and this realization and rescue are the reasons. I whisper a prayer of thanks for the rescue and the rescuer.

This unexpected connection with a stranger and the rush to survive heightens my emotions and feelings in the remote wilderness.

The stranger's arms tighten around my weak body, grounding me in reality. It's odd how, as my body weakens, my mind awakens, as if it is rallying to live.

Mak—Stay Awake! Please, God, don't let me die this close to being rescued!

As we navigate the wintry wilderness, my hypothermic state blurs with the warming tingle from my rescuer's embrace. I'm not merely holding on to the snowmobile—I'm clutching my new determination to break free from the grip of my broken engagement and the sadness of my first holiday without my parents.

God, I promise I will begin living the life I deserve—the one you've granted me with the gifts you've given me! I silently promise, feeling liberated, my mind clear, and the tension dissipating from me into the dark, swirling cold behind us.

I'm alive, and I won't waste this opportunity!

My grip weakens with this revelation, and my fingers slide off the handlebars.

Sensing my drifting consciousness, my rescuer pats me gently to keep me focused on the situation and awake. He holds me tighter, whispering unidentifiable but comforting words the wind snatches from me.

When I can't hold on or stay awake any longer, my cabin appears through the white walls around us.

Summoning every ounce of strength, I lift my arm, pointing. My body shakes with coldness and relief.

"Thank God!" I utter aloud.

He sees my gesture and expertly maneuvers us to the front.

I close my eyes and let my head fall back as we stop at the cabin. I want to untangle myself from his grasp and rush inside to warm up. However, my stiff, cold limbs refuse to cooperate, and moving is impossible.

My labored breathing and chattering teeth break the snowy silence. I try to release my grip on the handlebars, but my frozen fingers barely respond, leaving me hunched over the snow mobile's handlebars. I panic.

My mind assesses my current physical state. *I might be closer to hypothermia than I thought!*

Sensing my struggle, he bends down, assisting me in removing my hands from the grips, finger by finger. He lifts and pivots my legs to sit on the side of the snowmobile. Then he helps me stand by holding me at the waist and hoists me up like I move my immobile patients in the hospital.

His small actions reveal his strength and experience. *Does he work in healthcare? A Physical Therapist, perhaps?*

It fits. He is taller than me but slimmer and maneuvers and lifts me with a practiced ease.

My mind scrambles to piece together a coherent question, but my attention remains focused on the orange door and my critical need to reach it. The questions I long to ask are lost in the urgency of my need for warmth, shelter, and the comforting embrace of a heated room beyond the inviting door.

Stumbling towards the cabin, he supports me with his steady arms. He's not much taller than me, though he's strong and quick. My feet trip us, and he bends down and pulls me into his arms to carry me the rest of the way to the door.

My numb fingers fumble, pulling the keys in my pocket.

Why did I lock the door in wintertime? There's not a soul in sight for miles around this remote cabin.

Miraculously, I retrieve them. With sheer willpower, I unlock the door, as I can't feel my fingers, and my hazy vision leads my fingers to grasp the correct key, put it into the lock, and then turn it.

With the cabin's protection from the howling wind washing over us, he supports me as I stumble inside. My body is still waging a frosty rebellion to my commands.

His unwavering grip reassures me, and I crumple my face into his shoulder as he carries me to the center of the one-room cabin, where a couch awaits. The air fills with his scent of vanilla and the masculine scent of machine oil. His aroma awakens my senses, and I note the warmth of his breath on my neck.

It sends butterflies fluttering around my stomach and ending in a location lower in my abdomen.

My remote family cabin is a cozy, rustic retreat deep in the Alaskan wilderness. It's a wooden A-frame structure with a steep, snow-covered roof, allowing snow to slide off during heavy storms easily. The cabin is surrounded by tall pine trees, creating a picturesque, secluded setting. Inside, it's furnished with warm, comfortable furniture and a wood-burning stove that keeps the space toasty during the long, cold Alaskan winters. The windows offer panoramic views of the snow-covered landscape, and there's a well-stocked kitchen and bookshelf. This cabin is my place of solace and holds cherished family memories.

He carries me, rescuing me and delivering me to the cozy in a winter cabin. This scene is from a romantic holiday special starring my foxy rescuer and me. *Two strangers brought together by a twist of fate on Christmas Eve, stranded inside a cozy cabin, near death, while a blizzard rages outside . . .*

I shake my head. *Mak, wake up!*

Gently, he places me on the couch, then turns to close the door before expertly tending to the woodstove.

With each passing second, my body regains sensation, and my mind sharpens.

Thanks to his quick actions of warming me on the ride and getting me to shelter, I'll survive. My doctor's brain takes over, assessing the hypothermic patient—*me*. Sensation returns to all my limbs, and sharp daggers of pain shoot through my toes and fingers.

Pain is a welcome sensation—*More,* it's a sign my body is functioning. *I'm going to be okay.*

He ignites the fire in the woodstove, and the dancing orange light washes over the room, dispelling the darkness masking his face. His features are sharp but soft in a ruggedly handsome way with high cheekbones, intense brown eyes with long lashes, glowing, rosy cheeks, and a long, lean neck.

Holy Mother of all Rescuing Saints!

I move my hand to my medallion, reminding myself I just thanked and promised to follow God's plan minutes ago. And God rescued me from the storm and brought me together with this striking, strong person for a reason.

Before me stands a stunning *woman*!

Her features are balanced and captivating without makeup and handsome. The revelation leaves me frozen in awe, an unexpected twist sending a shiver down my spine. I rub my eyes in disbelief.

My rescuer moves with graceful precision, each action purposeful as she approaches the hooks and bench at the front door, shedding layers of snow gear. She removes her helmet and hat.

A gasp escapes my lips as she lifts it away, and her beautiful brown, tousled hair springs out.

Is this real? Am I imagining the woman of my dreams saving me?

I narrow my eyes, my chest tightening. *Perhaps I am hypothermic, lying in the snowy ditch, dying.*

I sigh. I'm satisfied with this ending if this is my dying hallucination.

I don't love Bryant because Bryant isn't the man in my romantic fantasies. My fantasies are of *women* and a fearless woman, *precisely* like my rescuer.

I smile, *God knows my truth,* and close my heavy eyelids.

I've died!

Chapter 4

Mak

My shaking body wakes me.

How long was I asleep?

Uncontrolled shivers race through me on the couch, and I clutch the blanket for warmth.

The grumbles of my rescuer's curses catch my attention, and I strain to hear her husky voice. The wind stole her soothing words earlier, and hearing her fierceness captivates me.

Her voice isn't the melodic, tender voice I expect from my protector in the blizzard—her voice is pragmatic, Alaskan, direct, and no-nonsense.

Who is she, and why was she out on Christmas Eve in this storm?

My rescuer checks her phone, frustration etched on her face. She reaches for the old-fashioned landline on the counter. "No service and no damn dial tone. This storm knocked everything out. Not that anyone could reach us out here anyway."

Her simple statement underscores our situation's gravity. This cabin is our only refuge from the raging storm outside the window, and I'm teetering on the brink of hypothermia. We're screwed if I don't warm up quickly.

"Are you okay? Are you injured? Can you feel your hands and feet?" Her voice softens as she fires questions at me.

I gaze back at her. The gratitude swelling within me at her saving me outweighs my discomfort. I choke and cough, saying, "I don't know." My voice sounds weak, even to my ears.

Moving to the wood stove, she stokes the fire, casting a warm glow across the room. Then, she tends to the propane heater, deftly adjusting the valve and lighting it with a match.

"Do you have any more wool blankets?" she asks.

"Yes," I reply, nodding towards the chest in the cabin's corner.

She retrieves the blankets from the chest and settles closely beside me, her eyes lock with mine. She's hot, confident, and dangerously attractive, flexing her large hands and pushing her fingers through her short brown curls.

"There." She gently presses the blankets around me, and my heart flutters. Unbeknownst to me, tears are on my cheeks, and she wipes them away with a tissue.

A few years older than me and taller. It's more than her height, making me smaller. I study her sharp features, illuminated by the soft flicker of the firelight.

"Better?" she asks, her intense brown gaze melting mine as she kneels before me. She dabs my cheeks gently with a tissue, her closeness stealing my breath.

I nod in response, as my mouth doesn't feel functional enough to ask her questions, and she turns back to tending the fire.

She begins, "I s'pose I ought to give you a proper introduction. My name's Pauline, but call me Paul. I'm trans, so I use the pronouns he and him." He glances at me, gauging my reaction.

"I'm Mak." Those few words are all I can say before my jaw jitters and a round of shivers goes through me.

"I was out on my propane delivery route—my work—when I spotted you. Army's my background. I'm wired to deal with any scenario, especially survival."

I stay quiet. My frozen neurons aren't firing fast enough for a reply. Luckily, he's not waiting for one and continues.

"Honestly, I wasn't plannin' on heading home. I'm a fuckin' mess and useless outside the military. I'm a drag on my folks," he shrugs. His gaze shifts back to me, and he absently rubs the back of his neck, a grimace crossing his face as if revealing too much.

He stands abruptly, moves to the entry, and sheds his remaining heavy boots and Carhart work overalls, revealing his lean and athletic physique. My gaze lingers on him, and my heart races. His strength and beauty captivate me, and though I see despondent patients in the Emergency Room, I cannot fathom why he'd consider such a desperate act.

The only thing that comes out of my mouth is a raspy "Thank you for helping me."

Paul's eyes meet mine, and there's a brief pause before he speaks, his words measured and direct. "I served in the military, deployed overseas to a war zone. I've seen things. Things *no one* should ever have to see. It changed me in ways I can't describe. I thought I could leave it all behind when I got home, but the memories haunt me."

My heart aches for the pain he's endured. "PTSD," I whisper, understanding the weight of those four letters. *I've treated patients with it, but coming face-to-face and being rescued by someone with PTSD is unexpected.*

Paul nods, his eyes holding mine. "I'll keep talking. *You* stay awake."

I realize he's being vulnerable to keep me engaged and listening. *It's working*—I want to know more about him. "Deal," I say.

He continues, sharing his inner struggles and reasons for seeking solitude in the wilderness. "It's a daily battle, trying to make sense of it all. I needed to escape the world, the expectations, the judgmental stares, my parents' disappointment, and my own perceived shortcomings. I had to get away. But *you*," he adds with a crooked smile and a light chuckle, "you ruined my plan."

I offer a reassuring nod and cock my head listening.

"I couldn't leave you out there to freeze. And here we are, against all odds, alive," he reflects.

I reach out and gently touch his arm, offering a wordless gesture of support. "I'm glad you found me," I say, "And thank you for warming me up and talking to me. You're braver and stronger than you realize."

Paul presses his lips together, turning to the fire. "Not strong enough. I couldn't save my platoon, stay in the army, or even watch fireworks tonight without freaking the fuck out."

The fire crackles, casting dancing shadows on the walls, and the storm outside rages on.

He sits by me on the futon, and my heart thumps with newfound sensations. His chest is broad and flat, which added to my assumption that he was a man during our snowy journey. His physique, one of someone accustomed to manual labor, defied conventional expectations.

I've never experienced an attraction like this, as my demanding medical studies limited my dating experience. The odd and exhilarating feelings are fizzing and popping inside me, creating a frenzy to discover more.

With my tummy fluttering and cheeks flushing, I examine his bare arms and strong shoulders. His heavy black tattoos represent his uniqueness, and the scars narrate his past. I yearn to hear the stories behind each one, to understand who he truly is, and *know* him.

I yearn to trace his contours with my finger and explore the heat building within me. Yet, my warming body steals my heat and causes me to hold my breath. My thoughts are foggy, and forming a coherent question is daunting with my unusual, electrifying attraction.

Thankfully, he maintains his gentle banter, a soft melody to calm me. He gracefully moves about as he speaks, starting the kettle and adding logs to the crackling fire.

I consider sharing with him a piece of my own journey, the darkness that consumed me after my parents' passing, the sense of isolation and loss. I want him to know that there's room for change, even when it feels like despair will never fade. For me, the healing process began here, in my parents' cabin, accepting they were gone and deciding I must live for myself, carrying their love.

I twist my mother's engagement ring that Bryant had once slipped onto my finger. It's different being alone, as I always had my parents and Bryant. Without my family, I don't have the connection and big holiday plans with a meal, presents, and festivities I'd had in years past.

But being at the cabin with Paul, my holiday sadness is lighter.

Could it be God who brought this person into my life to offer a connection to the world?

He leans closer, his voice quieting as he notices my eyelids drooping and my body struggling to stay awake. "What else do you need?"

You! But the words don't escape my lips. I'm utterly drained from the emotions of my crash, my near death, the surprising rescue by my dream partner, and my gratitude for being alive with him at my cabin.

Instead, I manage a weak "Thank you. I'm okay now." I give a smile to alleviate the concern etched around his eyes.

"You're still cold," he says, touching my cheek. "I've got to defrost you." He pokes the fire and tucks the blanket closer to my body. "The kettle is on for tea to thaw you out."

"Please don't leave," I say, moving to hold his hand, desperate to connect with him and afraid he will be gone forever if he leaves my side. I can't shake the feeling this is a hallucination, and I'm dying. *I don't want to be alone.*

He sits close, holding my hand in his large, warm hand. As the heat floods the small cabin, my shivers gradually subside, and my hands and feet throb and tingle. I gasped at the sensation of the heat penetrating.

He says, "I'll hold you to warm you up faster. Is that okay?"

I give a slight nod. My mouth is suddenly dry, and a deep desire awakens within me, the longing to be touched and held by him. My devious mind remakes the Hallmark movie to include a foot rub and tea.

Paul doesn't hesitate, enfolding us both in the woolen blankets, recreating the snug embrace we shared on the ride here. His long arms wrap around me, dispelling the numbness and replacing it with a comforting warmth.

Involuntarily, I inch closer, savoring Paul, my eyes closing as I breathe deeply and surrender into the embrace.

"Thank you for sharing your story," I say, looking up into Paul's firm, intense eyes.

Paul's brown eyes blink hard. "I wanted you to understand . . . with losing my platoon, my hometown not understandin' me, and my parents' burden . . . that's why I was out tonight, and if you don't live, then I'll probably head right back out that door."

"Sorry. I'm going to live. I can't let my rescuer go back out into the blizzard," I say and snuggle further into Paul, wiggling my arms from my sides to wrap around him, embracing him tightly back.

"Umph," he says, a warm breath ruffling my hair. "You're beautiful," he whispers.

I lean back to look into his soft eyes, and his lips part slightly, with his tongue darting out to wet them.

"You are beautiful, too," I say. The words escape before I can second-guess myself. Doubt crosses my mind: *did I choose the right word? Could it be perceived as an insult to this rugged Alaskan transgender man?*

The screeching kettle shatters the fragile, passionate atmosphere. He stands abruptly and, with brisk efficiency, rummages through cupboards for mugs, honey, and tea bags. "You warmin' up?"

Should I say, 'No,' so he returns to the couch and holds me again?

"I think so ... but ... I still feel frozen," I reply, looking at his inked, solid arms pouring the kettle.

Paul returns, setting the tea on the table beside me. "The hot tea will warm you up."

I move and successfully take a drink, my body finally complying with my brain and not too shaky. Paul isn't sitting as closely, so I move the blankets and scoot alongside him. "I'm still feeling a bit cold," I say with a smile, then I bite my lip and look up at him, batting my lashes.

He smiles and shakes his head. "I'll keep you close, *just* to raise your body temp. You keep drinkin' tea," he orders, his words carrying an authoritative tone, one I'm familiar with from scolding my patients in the emergency department.

I nod, pressing my lips together as I move closer to his open arms and welcoming embrace.

Lifting the blankets, Paul nestles me in a warm, secure embrace, enveloping me. Warmth courses through me as my body awakens, rekindling more than my cold skin. He ignites the internal flame of my dormant passion.

I'm uncertain if it's the crackling fire's warmth or the electric connection between us, but butterflies flutter, and my skin flushes. I've never wanted to be naked with another person as much as I do in this moment, and desire coursing through my veins.

With Bryant, I never felt anything like this. The passion and the need to be near him were absent. And this new passion of fluttering wings explodes from my core, pushing my blood to pound in my ears, and I'm barely able to stop shaking with excitement.

"You are still cold," he says, holding me tighter as I wiggle.

In the cozy, one-room cabin, its log walls adorned with hand-sewn quilts, our attraction burns brighter than the flickering fire. Paul's arms embrace me, his firm, solid body pressing against my softer, more petite frame, the stark contrast intensifying our magnetic connection.

His touch against my dark skin sends shivers of desire coursing through me. I nestle into him on the plush red knitted blanket beneath us, the soft cushions of the couch cradling our entangled bodies. The intimate atmosphere created by the gentle glow and our closeness heightens the urgency of my desire.

Is it the brush with death or the irresistible allure of my rescuer that ignites this fiery passion within me? I'm not sure, but I no longer wish to resist it.

Silently, Paul remains holding me, his comforting presence unwavering. With a gentle shift, he lays and envelopes me in his arms, making me the little spoon in our embrace. His strong legs intertwine with mine, and the thick wool blankets warmly cocoon us. Our breathing synchronizes, each inhale bringing us closer as my yearning intensifies with every slow exhale pressing my body further into his.

"I'm glad you're thawing out," Paul murmurs, his touch traveling from my lower abdomen up my side, grazing my ribcage and tracing the contours of my face. Our eyes lock, and the world outside fades away. Only the two of us are inside the cabin with the blizzard surrounding us.

Unable to resist the swelling explosion within me, I turn, facing Paul's solid body, my chest pressed against his and my brown eyes looking into his soft brown eyes. Desire courses through me, no longer hidden or repressed, and I'm drawn to Paul with an overwhelming hunger.

Paul's blackened wide pupils and quickening breath mirror my passion. I lean in to taste his lips.

Our lips meet in a fiery kiss that speaks of the passion we've discovered. I want more, and I'm not inclined to slow down.

"Whoa, Mak, we need to slow down and talk," Paul says.

I ignore Paul's cautious voice, filled with reason, that's attempting to intervene. I'm beyond the point of restraint. My tongue seeks entrance to his sweet mouth, and his response is fireworks.

Our kiss deepens, our tongues dancing in a slow, sensual exploration. There's no room for my Catholic shame or guilt in this intimate space, just an overwhelming sense of connection and longing. Our bodies press against each other, every inch vibrating with energy and heat.

As the intensity builds, our gazes remain locked, and anticipation prickles my skin. The fire crackles in the background, but all I can hear is the rapid beat of our hearts.

I pause, my lips hovering over Paul's, our eyes locked in a silent agreement. Then, I nip his bottom lip playfully, a teasing smile tugging at the corners of my mouth. The heat inside me explodes, and the sensations consume me. And our lips meet again in a passionate kiss.

The raging blizzard, Bryant, my sad holiday are forgotten. In this cabin, in the warmth of my desire, I'm alive and lost in a moment I've yearned for my entire life.

"Still want to slow down, Paul," I murmur through a playful smile, stealing his bottom lip. I stick out my tongue to trace his lip lightly, and his eyes dilate from the honey-brown to a ravenous black.

Chapter 5

Paul

I close my eyes, trying to find my balance, my lip throbbing and hot from her teeth and tongue. The kiss lingers, electrifying the small cabin as desire courses through us. Mak's warmth, passion, and longing are infused in her demanding kisses. The blizzard brought us together, but our need and passionate connection are more than surviving this deadly storm.

My eyes devour her stunning, captivating features with the soft glow bathing her profile: a smoldering expression in her rich dark chocolate eyes, her naturally red pouty lips, her creamy smooth coffee skin, and a soft round jaw surrounded by thick, shiny raven hair.

As I study her, Mak traps her bottom lip under her white nipping teeth and flutters her long lashes, making me groan.

She's not playing fair, and I don't want to take advantage of the woman I just rescued!

The urgency to warm her freezing body is fading, but there's another dangerous urge to take her in my arms and consume every part of her.

Mak's hands move to my chest, and I feel the warmth radiating from her, even with the layers separating us.

The small but pesky detail remains—a tight binder wrapped around my chest. As I lay against her, I'm acutely aware of this constriction, the fabric barrier separating us. My chest binder is a part of my identity, like the grease under my nails, and I wear it outside my home.

Not tonight! I want to show her everything and reveal myself to her.

She moves her hand over mine, tugging at the soft binder's seam. With hesitant fingers, her eyes meet mine as she slowly unravels the binding tightly holding me. With the binder off, she pulls the tight tank top over my head and shifts to kiss the imprinted lines around my ribs. And her lips move to kiss the scars scattered across my body.

Her kisses make my skin flush, my heart beats even harder, and a moan escapes my lips at her touch. I run my fingers through her dark hair, relishing the softness and silkiness of each strand.

"Paul," Mak says breathless from our kisses, her voice trembling and her eyes soft, "I want you."

Her words spark an unexpected tenderness in hear-ing her words' want, acceptance, and desire and the fiery hunger in her eyes. Mak's hands find their way beneath my shirt, our remaining clothing becoming a barrier, and I shiver at her touch.

My fingers trail down her back, and warmth flows from my racing heart through my fingertips as they graze her rich, soft, coffee-colored skin. Her heartbeat is steady and reassuring as she quivers under me amid the frigid storm raging through the windows. I trace the curves of her cool body, and her wet clothing sticks to my fingers.

Damn, I made a mistake! I left her in her snow-drenched attire, sapping away her heat.

I kick myself for the rookie mistake. I pull back slightly, looking into her eyes. "Mak, I should remove your wet clothes."

"Yes," she says without hesitation, reaching for the seam of her shirt.

My rough hands trace a path down her body, memorizing every luscious curve and perfect contour, leaving my fingertips tingling in her wake. Her skin is warm and soft—so soft my fingers feel like sandpaper in comparison. It's a stark contrast—the ruggedness of my battle-worn hands against the delicate lines of her body. Her smooth skin rests softly against the hard scars etched onto my torso.

My calloused hands chafe against her delicate skin as I quickly, but gently, remove her damp shirt. As I pull the cloth from her curvy body, my army medical training forces me to check for hidden injuries.

Her fingers move to her pink bra and unfasten the clasp to free herself. She looks at me, her eyebrows raised, and I smile back.

My fingers graze over the engagement ring on her finger, and I carefully adjust the medallion hanging from her neck, ensuring it doesn't catch on her pink bra as I assist her out of her shirt.

Questions whirl in my mind. *Is she unavailable? Where's her partner? Does she really want to be with me, or is this post-rescue horniness?*

I shake my head. *Stay focused! Don't get distracted by those curves.*

I want to ask about the ring, but as I catch my breath, I see the desire mirroring in her eyes. Instead, I ask, "Mak, are you sure?"

She nods, runs her finger lightly over my bottom lip, and looks deeply into my eyes. "I've never been more sure of anything in my life."

The fire crackles in the background, casting a warm, intimate radiance over us. The blizzard's relentless howling winds are replaced by the sweet sounds of our sighs and moans, the crackling fire a passionate soundtrack to our desires.

The small cabin fills with the sounds of our needs, passion, and the whispers of love. Mak makes me forget the world outside, the blizzard, the past, and my pain.

I exhale deeply, a weight released, and enjoy the harmony in this unexpected intimacy.

I'm not going back out into the storm.

Chapter 6

Paul

A jolt of cold pierces my body, startling me from sleep. My eyes flicker open, disoriented. *Where am I? And why does it feel like I'm holding an ice block?*

Peeking beneath the blanket, I find the source of this icy intrusion—*Mak's frozen feet* nestled against my leg. I suppress a yelp when a toe twitches, sending a cold shard through me.

Steady now. You've faced war—do not react. It's only a cold toe! I remind myself not to wake her with a sudden movement or shout.

I adjust the blanket, allowing the firelight to reveal her feet further, ensuring they're not frostbitten.

Nope, they're pink—surprisingly cute, albeit cold, for this very hot woman, and the pink painted toenails make me want to kiss her sweet frozen toesies.

The pink makes me smile as I remember her pink panties and bra, which I now think are *entirely appropriate* Alaska winter gear.

As she stirs and snuggles closer, her icy feet move to a new home on my warm calves.

Unbelievable! But it's hard to be mad at such a lovely woman. Suppressing another yelp, I remind myself she *was hypothermic* not too long ago. *And keeping her warm is my mission for the night.*

I tighten the blanket around us, creating a barrier between her frozen toes' icy attacks and my warm legs. I settle into our spooning embrace, and an unfamiliar, comfortable intimacy warms me.

The sensation of her against me goes beyond physical heat as it melts the icy walls around my heart. I never expected to be comforted in the arms of an unknown woman, yet *here I am,* drawn into this unexpected connection with *her.*

However, lingering questions rather than nightmares prevent sleep from claiming me. *Why is she wearing an engagement ring? Who is she?*

"Why are you here on Christmas, not with your fiance?"

She cracks open her eyes and softly answers, "Umm? What did you ask, Paul?"

"Why aren't you spending Christmas with your family?" I ask, amending my question.

"I don't have family anymore. My parents are gone and being here reminds me of past holidays with them."

I nod.

"I guess we are both stuck with the ghosts of Christmas Past," she says and nestles closer, her feet trying to bypass the blanket.

Her words resonate, and I have spent too much time with my ghosts. Holding and talking with her last night makes me want to try living again. An involuntary smile tugs at my lips, and she meets my gaze, returning the smile.

"I'm happy," I respond.

"The perks of rescuing women," she says. She sighs and wiggles further into my warm frame as I wrap my arms around her.

"Actually," I murmur, my voice filled with tenderness. "Thank *you* for giving me . . ." Words fail me.

Her hand grazes my cheek, and her eyes crease with her deep affection. She moves closer, her body pressing against mine, her lips tantalizingly close. "A reason to live?" she finishes for me.

"Yeah," I say. "I said last night. You might not remember."

She turns, pushes the blanket barrier away, and presses her body against mine. "I remember."

Our bodies remain entwined, facing each other, our warm breath mingling in the cabin's stillness. The crackling fire casts playful shadows on the walls, setting the scene. Our vulnerability binds us in our raw embrace, and she nestles her head on my chest.

As her breathing steadies, a sense of unease creeps in, tightening my gut, and my warm feelings dissipate with the fading firelight. Despite my asking about her family, she's not mentioned her engagement ring and relationship status.

I don't want to ask directly and shatter our new connection, but I *must* know. *Is this real? Does she care about me? Can we have a future together?*

In the midst of my internal struggle, she stirs from her sleeping state, her arm instinctively curling around my shoulder, pulling me closer. Her warmth soothes the raw edges of my uncertainty. Her breath caresses my neck, and I breathe her scent and warmth.

I focus on her, not letting my mind wander into darker territory. Our fingers meet, and I relish the softness of her touch, the genuine tenderness. I allow myself to savor the comfort of her body against mine, the rhythm of her breathing, and the gentle brush of her lips on my shoulder.

Our connection is *real, tangible, and undeniable. This* is what matters.

With a determined exhale, I close my eyes and slow my chest to synchronize my breathing. My heart beats faster even as my breath slows. As my VA counselor taught me, I let my breath out and slowly let another in, holding it and releasing it.

I *will* not let my mind wander along its usual dark paths.

Tomorrow, I'll ask her about the ring and be open to whatever truth she tells me. My arm tightens around my cold little spoon as sleep claims me.

Tomorrow!

Chapter 7

Mak

The first rays of sunlight gently coax me awake, their golden tendrils weaving warm ribbons throughout the cabin. Carefully, I extract myself from the comfort of the bed, not wanting to disturb Paul. He lies peacefully sleeping, a serene but tough figure.

I sigh and quietly ensure the woolen blanket is snugly wrapped around his enticing body, a silent gesture to protect him as he protected me last night.

Stepping gingerly across the creaking wooden floor, I make my way to the wood stove. Its radiant warmth brings back fond memories of our passionate night, and I tend to the embers, nurturing the flames that ignited our desire.

My gaze drifts across the room to Paul. I contemplate the queer feelings swirling within me—lust, need, and an overwhelming sense of comfort in his embrace. I have a foreign, physical craving that defies all logic and reason.

Was it the brush with death that compelled me to acknowledge my long-hidden desire?

My fingers trace the St Michael medallion around my neck, a gift from Marianne, my biggest cheerleader since my mom's passing. It's a reminder of God's protection over me and the Catholic values instilled in me from a young age.

During his enlistment, my father wore a similar medallion of Saint George, which protected him during the war. He was a devout man of few words, and he rarely discussed the trauma he endured. His hidden pain and the unshakeable shadow of his past fueled my desire to become a Psychiatrist and help people confront their inner demons.

Last night's events were *most definitely not* within the Catholic teachings or my upbringing. A flush burns through me, and I move my hand quickly from the medallion, my mom's ring tangling in the chain.

The ring reminds me of the upcoming task of getting Bryant out of my life. Last night reinforced my decision: I'm not getting back with Bryant. But he hasn't moved out or moved on because I haven't made it public yet. I can't bear to disappoint Marianne and my coworkers.

What would Marianne and the St Mary's staff think about my unorthodox relationship?

The thought alone is enough to make me queasy. No doubt coming out could cost me my job. St. Mary's Hospital is deeply rooted in Catholic teachings, guided by bishops, and bound by policies that align with the Church's doctrine. They won't perform life-saving pregnancy terminations or prescribe birth control to unwed women.

I look away from Paul and into the crackling flames. The thought of losing my job and the ensuing rumors churns the acid in my stomach.

I move to rid myself of the stress by tidying. As I move about the room, gathering discarded clothing, my fingers brush against something hard in the inner pocket of Paul's jacket. Curiosity gets the better of me, and I reach inside, retrieving a familiar item—an Epi-Pen.

My stealthy snooping fails when the EpiPen tumbles to the ground with a clatter echoing loudly in the cabin.

Oh, no!

Chapter 8

Paul

My eyes snap open, and my body tenses at the sharp nearby sound. My heart races, my head pounding, and the scent of ash instantly overtakes me. *Fuckin' PTSD!* I can't shift gears with my body yelling at me to fight or take cover.

Mak quickly moves, placing a calming hand on my shoulder, which helps ground me to the cabin and her. My heartbeat slows.

"Paul, it's okay. You're safe," she reassures me. "Take a deep breath with me, in ... and out." She takes a slow breath, and I follow her lead.

She continues her gentle guidance, helping to alleviate the panic gripping me. Gradually, my racing heart slows, and the pounding in my head subsides. The smell of ash fades into the background until I only smell the wood fire and Mak's sweet scent.

Calmer, I meet Mak's wide, golden-brown eyes tentatively locking onto mine, and I remind myself *I'm still alive in a remote cabin with the gorgeous woman I rescued last night.*

"Merry Christmas," I manage with a small smile. Despite the startled wake-up, there's a pleasant hum in my body. And I haven't had restorative sleep in weeks.

Mak's tousled long hair is fanned across her shoulders as she bites her plump lower lip. *An attractive bedmate might have contributed to my good night's rest.*

"Merry Christmas," she replies, her voice quiet as she moves away to finish gathering my scattered belongings and hangs my jacket by the door.

Does she regret last night?

"What's the epi-pen for?" she asks.

I furrow my brows, wondering at the change of conversation and coolness in the air between us.

"I should have said-I'm a doctor. I work in the Emergency Department with mental wellness. It's automatic, asking invasive health questions," she continues, with a hint of playfulness.

My heart skips a beat at her smile. Her revelation of being a doctor surprises me, but in hindsight, *it makes sense.* She's caring and certainly knows her way around a body. Her professional-like listening skills and compassion should have given away her job.

"I'm deathly allergic to lavender, and ginger, and there's a few other random things I'm mildly allergic to. My worst allergy is from Benadryl, of all things. So I keep an EpiPen with me," I explain.

Mak is like a truth serum. I can't lie to her piercing, kind eyes. Besides, seeing her in a tight tank top stretching dangerously over her curves, outlining her nipples, steals my breath away. *I'd tell her anything!*

"Really?" She turns to face me, her brow raised. Her deep cleavage and the light tracing her body steal the air from the room, and my heart pumps in overdrive.

Damn!

I glance away. The snow outside has stopped. Then I add, "My parents don't have allergies. I'm just unlucky. I had to keep an allergy journal to determine what soaps, chemicals, and foods triggered me."

"Your allergist is very patient to help you figure it out," she replies and returns to sit with me on the futon.

"My mom did it all. She's amazing!"

She places her hand over mine, and her eyes sparkle. "I wouldn't want you to have an emergency in the middle of nowhere." She laughs and moves the blankets to snuggle against me.

My cheeks flame at her jest. Her soft contours fit into my hard angles, and I wrap my arms around her, *my little spoon.* A lingering longing relaxes me, but the harsh morning wake-up leaves me with a bittersweet ache.

How could a stunning doctor be interested in a filthy, messed-up mechanic?

She sits up. "I'll whip up some toast or something."

I smile and nod. With my emotions brewing, I decided to break my vow. *I am not asking about the ring.* I want to enjoy being with her before reality sets in.

She squeezes my hand and interlaces her fingers with mine. Then she brings my hand up to her mouth to lightly kiss it as she gets up.

Her soft lips on my hand make me freeze.

Say something, soldier! Don't be creepy!

"Err ...," I clear my suddenly dry throat. "I could eat."

She heads to the kitchen, starting the kettle.

"I have an idea for a rural veterans' support group. Village patients can't attend in-person sessions and my dad, a veteran himself, found peace staying out here in Caribou Hills. People shouldn't have to leave the peaceful countryside to go into the busy city for care."

I frown, shaking my head, more startled at the conversation change than seeing her pink underwear over her voluptuous butt.

Damn! "You want me in therapy?"

I move quickly to put on my binder and an oversized sweatshirt, not wanting to reveal any more of myself to *the doctor.*

Does she see me as a broken soldier or her lover?

"No. . .I mean, yes, but when *you are ready.* I was thinking aloud. Sorry, I need to turn off my professional brain. You're my friend, and I want you to be happy. Let me make you breakfast, okay?"

I look away, avoiding her gaze and hiding my hurt as I realize our passionate encounter was her way of comforting me and more of a one-night stand than an invitation to a relationship. I'm just *her friend.*

Mak moves further away, giving me some privacy while she keeps herself busy. She says, "Actually, I'll make you my famous breakfast sandwich and coffee, *stat.*"

"You had me at coffee," I respond weakly, but I must get out of this cabin and away from her.

She grins, oblivious to the mood change. "It's a toasted bacon, banana, peanut butter, and honey sandwich on sourdough bread. An *Elvis specialty*, you'll love it!"

I have already found something I love, and it's not food.

She continues talking while working in the kitchen."I expected to be alone. I only have comfort food here. But, if I was dying or on death row, this is the meal I'd pick."

I nod, folding the blankets and trying not to stare at her shapely butt.

"What would you request as your last meal?" she asks, toasting sourdough bread in a frying pan next to the thick, peppered bacon. The savory scent fills the small space, and my stomach rumbles louder, betraying me.

I might as well eat and be friendly. "I'd pick an overnight, slow-cooked pulled pork with Frito pie and sweet tea," I respond.

She laughs, and her chest jiggles.

My heart flutters more. She's not mentioning anything about our future or the wedding ring. I look out the window. "Are you ready to head out soon?"

"Sure. I have to work this evening," she says, pouring coffee and plating the sandwiches, then setting them on the table by the futon.

I sit and take a big bite. "Mmmm."

"Good, right?"

I nod and polish off the sandwich and coffee in record time.

"I'll drop you at the gas station and Jim'll get you set up with a tow or ride to Anchorage."

She nods and takes our plates as I get up, throwing on my snow gear.

I wish she'd asked me to drive her or say *anything* to indicate she wants to be more than a friend or a doctor referring me to therapy.

She stays silent, tidying the cabin.

"I need to get back and let my parents know I'm okay," I add. I open my phone and quickly send a message. My parents were probably worried sick as I didn't check in with them last night.

"Hey, Paul." She looks at me with her deep brown eyes. "If I didn't say it, thank you for rescuing me." She pulls me into a long, tender embrace.

I accept the embrace and hold her close for a few seconds. Trying not to enjoy it or imagine it means anything more than it does.

"I need to warm up the snowmobile. I'll see you out there," I say, excusing myself and exiting abruptly.

If I don't leave her now, I'll never leave. And she clearly doesn't have room for me in her life. I'm a headcase to her. *Broken!*

Chapter 9

Mak

"Mak! Doctor Makayla Jackson, I need you here. Now!" Nurse Jessica's voice slices through the tranquility of the Emergency Department, jolting me from my daydream. I slam my computer closed, hiding the tabs opened on the browser: St Mary's employee's morality clause—*Employees must follow the Catholic teachings*— PTSD counselors in Ninilchik—*There's none*—and checking Paul's social media—*He has no accounts.*

My daydream of seeing Paul again is ruined by the harsh reality of work pulling me back into the present, where I'm a respected doctor in a bustling *Catholic* hospital.

I wasn't the rational choice for the position. Still, my mom's friend recommended me, and "I fit in with the St Mary's culture," according to the hospital hiring committee, which refers to me being a St. Mary's Catholic Church parish member.

My magical night with Paul replays in my mind like a catchy jingle on an endless loop throughout my day. Falling for someone like Paul doesn't fit this hospital's old-fashioned culture. He's not a rational choice—but my heart doesn't care what's sensible and that the relationship could cost me my job.

Worse than that is the guilt of using work to escape Paul and the discussion of our intimacy. I ran away without even getting his number or saying a proper goodbye. I retreated into the safety of the known, my doctor persona instead of acknowledging our connection and exploring the possibility of a future together.

I frown, walking through the sterile, white hallway, following the sound of nurse Jessica's voice. I weave through the department, where Christmas decorations adorn the walls, and the gentle strains of holiday tunes emanate from speakers. Amidst the medical apparatus and the constant beep of monitors, the nurses' station glimmers with stockings and garlands, a festive gesture for staff and visitors.

Jessica grabs and nudges me playfully, "You were bringing me a pen." She raises her eyebrows, and I sigh, handing her my pen. *I forgot.*

"I *swear,* if I didn't know you, I'd say you were twitter-pated," she teases, widening her blue eyes and waiting for my response.

I respond with a sheepish smile, attempting to suppress my thoughts. "No, I'm tired of doing *both* our work while you dance around to Christmas carols," I quip, smiling.

"Really? I saw your butt swaying along, too, Beyonce." She raises a perfectly arched eyebrow and pouts her glossy red lips at me.

I shake my head and grin. Whatever, Shakira!"

Working the same shift as my friend is a blessing, but focusing on working while she teases me and tries to figure out why my head is in the clouds is challenging.

Jess's infectious mood spreads, prompting a grin wider. I glance around cautiously, ensuring our conversation is private, before confessing, "I'm contemplating my future and someone special."

I chose my words carefully as I can't reveal my broken engagement before talking with Bryant or the new relationship consuming my thoughts. Jessica's open-minded, but what Paul and I share isn't conventional or expected from *me*. I've *never* indulged in a one-night stand *with a person like Paul, except in my secret fantasies.*

Jess leans in, giving my butt an affectionate pinch, her tone playful. "That's obvious. You're practically oozing sexual energy, girl."

"Stop!" I protest, my eyes darting around for eavesdroppers. We may be a Catholic hospital, but the gossip mill thrives, spreading faster than a glitter bomb.

She chuckles. "Yeah, right. You aren't a nun. You've had your fair share of workplace romances. Where *is* McDreamy? Did you get stuck in the supply closet with him while fetching me a pen?" She winks and nudges me.

"You know I don't discuss my personal life at work. Let's talk after shift." I shouldn't have hinted at my mood. This is not the place to talk about it or drop a truth bomb on her.

"Ooof. Try next week. I'm working doubles to cover."

I nod. Next week, allows me to sort out my feelings and talk with Bryant. By then, I will be public with our break-up, and he better be out of the house!

"Earth to Dr. Mak. You're daydreaming about Dr. McDreamy, aren't you?"

Her teasing is good fun, but I'm distracted and can't tell her the truth even though my glowing skin and constant smile hint at my secret.

Jess is my closest friend, yet I haven't told her the truth about my relationship—or the *lack thereof*—with our coworker, Bryant. She did *introduce us,* and I hate to burst her bubble on being a fantastic matchmaker. It's part of what initiated our friendship.

"You look more in love than ever. Seriously, Mak!"

I look around, ensuring there's no one to overhear us. *I can share a little. I need to tell someone!*

"I've had a few relationships before, but I've found it—the sweet, Hallmark romance we always joke about, you-know, the as-seen-on-TV passionate instant love."

Her eyes light up. "Ahh! It's a real Christmas miracle! You're lucky, Mak. You're starting your fabulous career, embarking on life with a *serious hottie*, and you look absolutely radiant. Love suits you!"

I bite my lip from correcting her assumption that I'm referring to Bryant. The nurses adore him. I want to confess about Paul and the lack of passion with Bryant, but I can't.

I nod and reply softly, mindful of the nearby secretary, "Thanks, Jessica. I appreciate you. I'm taking you on a coffee date next week."

Beneath the surface, I'm grappling with a more daunting dilemma of redefining my sexual identity and *when I will see Paul again.*

Also, what will happen if I reveal my non-traditional feelings and new relationship?

I'm already the newest doctor on staff, a minority as a female and Latino staff, and adding another label, especially one referring to my unusual sexuality, doesn't make me their ideal diversity hire- it makes me a sinner in the eyes of this Catholic establishment. I can envision my coworkers' sidelong glances, the rumors, and disdain.

Is being fired worth being honest and trying a relationship with Paul?

I love my job and the people I help. I touch the medallion from Marianne that reminds me of my father. My dad and mom were proud that I was a doctor working at St. Mary's. This *was* my dream—*our dream*—before I met Paul.

Chapter 10

Mak

"Hey, Mak, we need to talk." Jessica's voice slices through my concentration like a scalpel, making me jump a little. I quickly click, saving my notes on my bereaved patient's chart.

"Jess, what's up?"

She looks at her feet, then says, "There's some gossip in the Respiratory Department. People are saying your wedding is off."

Oh no!

I inhale quickly. "What? Who's spreading this rumor?"

Is it a coincidence the rumors have started from Bryant's department? Maybe he's finally accepting our break-up and telling people.

"Is it true?" She looks directly into my eyes.

The chaos of the Emergency Department is forgotten as I stand and motion for her to follow me to a quieter corner of the busy nursing station.

"Jess," I begin and bite my lip. I say in a lower tone, "Yes, it's true. Bryant and I aren't getting married."

She turns to me and touches my hand briefly. "What?"

I take a deep breath, my heart racing. "Bryant and I ... I broke off our engagement."

"What happened? You two are *perfect* together." Her rapid questions run together.

I'm unsure how much to reveal, but I *must* confide in someone, especially if the rumor mill is churning. *How am I going to contain or control this?*

I bite my lower lip, holding back the waves of emotion crashing over me as my heart pounds. "It wasn't right, Jess. We were pretending. I didn't love him, and *he* doesn't love me."

Her eyes widen, and she gasps. "Mak, are you serious?"

"There's more. The reason Bryant and I aren't getting married is—" I sigh, thinking of how to explain my feelings for Paul. "It's complicated."

She leans forward and touches my hand. "Complicated? Like how? Cheating? Pregnancy?"

I pause at her rapid-fire questions. "I'm not sure if I should say anything. I need to talk to Bryant."

Her hand moves to mine, and her eyes lock onto me. She says, "Mak, you know you can trust me. Whatever it is, I'm *your* friend."

"I know, Jess, and I appreciate you. But it's hard to explain and I need to talk with Bryant first. I think he's feeling jilted and doesn't want to give up on our relationship, even though it's been stagnant for a while. I need to have that conversation with him, and it's going to be tough. He's a great guy, but I have feelings for someone else. And this is about more than canceling the wedding. It might affect my job."

Her hand springs to her throat, and she scrunches her nose. "Whoa! Your job? What do you mean?"

I inhale deeply, steadying myself. Saying it aloud would make it real. But my friend deserves to know, and *I can't hold this back any longer.*

"There's something I haven't told you," I begin in a whisper. "In Caribou Hills, I didn't have snow tires and slid off the road and got stuck in my Jeep in a blizzard. And I thought I was going to freeze to death. It was terrifying, but it also made me evaluate my life."

My friend leans in, her expression softening. "And you came to work? I had no idea. Are you okay?"

I nod, and despite the seriousness, I smile softly, recalling the events of the last twenty-four hours. "Yes, I'm okay *now*. But here's the thing: as I was hypothermic and losing hope, praying, a miracle happened." I touch my pendant.

Her eyes widen, and she asks, "What kind of miracle?"

She must be surprised if she's not asking her usual five questions at once.

I take a breath. My voice trembles as I explain, "I was saved by a stranger who was also in a desperate situation. God threw us together, and it was a surreal situation. It's hard to describe." I shrug.

She touches my hand again and wordlessly waits for me to share more.

I grab her hand, and my heart flutters. "It was love at first sight like God answered my prayers. I was rescued, but there was more, a deep, instant connection between us."

I pause and shiver from the excitement coursing through me as I say, "It was everything I dreamed of when meeting my soulmate. Those romance novels we read and romcoms we watch together-it was just like that."

Her gasp fills the room, and her eyes widen more. "Mak, that's ... That's incredible! What about Bryant? Who is this new guy?"

Before I can answer, her brow furrows, and she says, "If you're not engaged to Bryant anymore, are you guys still living together? You know you are already pushing it, dating a coworker and then living together not married. The only reason the hospital board has ignored it is your relationship with Marianne."

I bite my lip and nod. "I know, Jess. That's the problem. Bryant was going to move out, and we were going to have a friendly, public breakup *after* the holidays."

She nods and holds my hands tight.

"Now, with this rumor, I have no clue what to do. I haven't talked to Bryant since my trip. I was reviewing the hospital's morality clause and I think I could lose my job."

She places a reassuring hand on my shoulder. "Mak, you've got to do what's right for you. You're a brilliant doctor, and there's no way the hospital will fire you," she says with conviction.

Then she adds, "The only person they've fired on the morality clause was a guy who turned out to be gay, so you have no worries. And the board is supposably trying to reflect the community by moving to be more inclusive."

I sigh and bite my lip. How do I tell her my soulmate is an amazing trans man? Would she still be my friend and stand by me if she knew?

My mind races with the situation's complexities—I need to talk to Bryant and make a plan, stat. The overhead speaker blares before I can ruminate further.

"Emergency Room 14. Code Blue. Code Blue. ER 14."

Chapter 11

Paul

My dad eases into the well-worn chair beside me and hands me the wrench for the truck without me even needing to ask. Taking the tool, I want to open up to him about my recent encounter and new feelings.

Pop and I share an unspoken connection, but lately, with my dark mood, we are distant. I want to bridge our gap but struggle to articulate my feelings.

"Pop," I begin, my words slow, "I'm doing some serious thinking. I can't help but feel like I'm missing something in my life, something—deeper." I shrug, with my pathetic attempt at explaining my emptiness and describing the recent fullness I felt with meeting Mak. My hand tucks her left-behind Santa hat deeper inside my cargo pants pocket.

Just touching it makes my heart thump, and I lick my lips.

His gaze meets mine. He nods and gives a knowing look that suggests he's attuned to the thoughts weighing on my mind. "Go on, Paul. I'm all ears."

I draw a deep breath, attempting to gather my thoughts into coherent words. "It's not that I'm unhappy here with you and Mom, per se. It's this shitty, aimlessness, like I'm stationary while traffic moves around me." I shrug. "I can't explain right, but I have this feeling I should be dead, not the one alive. But that's not it. There's something more."

I pause and don't say anymore. My words are flat.

Pop nods, his eyes crinkle in understanding, and he places his hand on my shoulder. "I get it, son. Life's path can be winding. We are *proud of you,* and it takes time to come home from the war."

I lean back in my chair, the weight of my contemplation heavy. "Yeah. I'm doing some soul-searching, trying to figure out what's missin'. Maybe it's time I connect- you know? With something or someone. A bigger purpose."

His smile is easy, and he squeezes my shoulder. "Paul, let me show you something." He reaches into his pocket and retrieves a weathered medal.

Something from his military days?

"This belonged to a dear friend of mine. He was a better man than me, but he's not here and *I am*. Friends and connecting is important. He helped me through rough patches and reminded me to focus on the good- you and your mom." He smiles and looks down at the piece of metal. "I strive to be the friend and man he saw me as."

He hands it to me.

I take the small medallion on the chain, and it's a dog tag but an image of a Saint imprinted into the metal. My finger traces the well-worn etching.

"Saint George. He's yours, to remind you, that *you are enough*. You survived, like me, and you deserve happiness," Pop's voice carries the weight of memory.

I swipe my teary eyes at his revelation. My dad avoids talking about his past, but I know this trinket must mean more to him than his displayed Medal of Honor since he carries it close.

"Thanks, Pop."

"Caribou Hills is a special place, and I moved here for the community and the wilderness. I was a mess when I came back to your mom after the war. I'd take off into the tundra, like you, trying to outrun my demons. Then I ran into an old friend who understood. We leaned on each other for support, for a connection. We ran in different circles, but I knew if I needed him, he had my six."

I wrap my hand around it and feel the significance, not in its physical weight but the meaning it holds to my Pop.

"What are you sayin'?"

He leans closer, his eyes searching. "Paul, sometimes the connection we seek isn't what we expect. Have the courage to let go of the past and step into the future with whoever has your back. You aren't alone."

"Pop, I can't take this."

"Yes, you can. And remember, me and your mom always have your back. You'll meet friends along the way. You're not alone, and you deserve to be alive," he says, putting his mitts over my fisted hand.

I absorb his words, recognizing the medal as the cherished symbol it is. Dad found this knowledge from his friend. Now, he's passing the wisdom to me—a bridge between generations, a link within my fisted hand.

My fingers rub the medal, and a peculiar sense of peace washes over me as the metal warms in my hand. "Pop, I'll cherish it. Thanks."

He nods and lets go of my hand.

I add, "I've met someone special who I connected with. It terrifies me."

He pats my shoulder, his eyes reflecting warmth. "I know. Good. I have no doubt you'll find your way. Remember, you're not alone."

He smiles, adding, "Maybe you'll even have a wonderful kid, like I did, someday."

"Ugh! Pops, don't ruin it!" I smile and cuff his shoulder.

As we sit there, my uncertainties are lighter, and a newfound connection fills me. I slip the medal into my pocket.

"Your mom's taking the ham out of the oven," he interrupts, suddenly looking at the door and remembering why he came out to the garage.

My mom will be hollering at us soon, no doubt.

I slide my tools out from under the truck and wipe my hands on my coveralls. "I was about to take a break, Pop. Perfect timing."

"How's Bob's truck coming along?" my dad asks, leaning over the truck as I put away the tools.

"It'll be purring like a damn beast once I'm done," I reply, giving the truck a solid pat.

"I've heard folks talking about hiring you for the municipality fleet. You're the go-to diesel mechanic in Ninilchik. I'm proud of you. Now, let's go eat," he says, patting my back and flashing me a brief smile.

"Thanks, Pops. Talking with you and working here is good."

"I know you had your sights set on leaving this small town," he says, "but it grows on you, right?"

Growing up, I couldn't wait to escape. I didn't have friends and didn't relate to the girls in my class who were engrossed in boys and fashion— I had a rough time growing up, but we don't discuss it much. Our conversations lean toward trucks, hunting, and guy topics I enjoy.

I nod.

He continues, "It's not so bad here. And I appreciate having you around to do the deliveries. Everyone in town likes having a diesel mechanic. You could do well staying."

"True," I say, pausing.

Mom must have put him up to trying to get me to stay, and I don't want to get her hopes up. There's no place, aside from the army, I've ever felt comfortable. I'm not gonna promise to stay, but at the same time, there's nowhere else for me.

My thoughts drift to Mak, her soft body curled warm against mine. She makes me want to stay, to have a home to share with her. The warm, comfy feeling of waking up next to her is more home-like than any location on a map. I could get used to that feeling.

I frown, sorting my tools. *Home with her is impossible.* This town's only good things are my parents and this garage.

My mom enters the shop from the house.

"I overheard you guys chatting. How about a break for early Christmas Dinner? You know most people take the day off, right?" she jokes.

"The work's gonna be waitin', either way," my pop and I say in unison.

We laugh, and my mom smiles wide, wiping her hands on her apron.

"Paul, that's the first time I've heard you laugh in a while. It sounds good." Her eyes shine, and she smiles at me.

I turn away, hiding the blush on my cheeks as I think about the reason I'm in good spirits-*Mak*.

My pop adds, "We can eat."

My mom's stern gaze fixes on me, her response blunt. "And Paul, you need to put some meat on those bones. I've got pecan pie *and* apple pie with ice cream ready."

I chuckle, raising my hands. "Alright, alright. I surrender. I'll eat."

"Can you even recall the last decent meal you had?" my pop quips, poking fun at me.

Without missing a beat, I reply, "An Elvis sandwich this mornin'."

My mom's eyebrows raise, and she asks, "What in the world is that?"

I shrug. "It's a mishmash of crispy bacon, peanut butter, bananas, and a drizzle of honey on sourdough bread," I explain, a grin tugging at the sides of my mouth.

My dad's eyes opened wide in surprise. "All together—in a sandwich?"

"Trust me. I'll make you one. You'll love it." Knowing his love for anything involving bacon, this will become his favorite sandwich. *Maybe his last meal request.*

"I'm pleased to hear that *you* want to cook," my mom ribs me, "I'll eat anything you make." My mom's warm smile lights up her features. "You do seem different—happier—since returning from your blizzard rescue this morning."

I gave my parents the abbreviated version of the story.

My dad nods in agreement, and I hide a smile once again. I'm getting used to laughing and grinning again.

My mom puts her hands in her apron. "Not to suggest you were unhappy before or you needed to change. We're your parents, and we only want the best for you."

"I know," I grumble, giving my mom a nudge with a clean part of my arm.

My mom looks down at my black hands. "Paul, you're a greasy mess!"

"I'll wash while you're settin' the table." I stride to the sink and reach for the industrial cleaner. "Gimme a sec. I'll be right out."

"Table's set. I'm waiting for you," my mom calls.

"Roger that. I'm on the way," I reply, saluting her before turning on the water.

"I forgot. I got you guys new shop supplies. I'll grab out the towels for your workbench." She goes to the cupboard.

My mom's the best. If smiling makes her happier, then I'll smile more. I *could* call my therapist and restart sessions. For Mom, I'll make time for the weekly phone call, and I have a feeling if I run into Mak again, she'll be happy to hear. She may track me down. Ninilchik is a tiny village, after all, and she was thinkin' to get me into that new rural PTSD group.

I wouldn't mind talking to her again. I smile. *I might need to track her down first.* I could always ask Jim where he had her Jeep towed to.

My parents are trying their best to help me, givin' me support and being there. My mom has gone above and beyond, feeding me, housing me, getting me back to work, doing laundry, and becoming my cheerleader. Even my pop transformed his garage to accommodate a diesel shop in it for me. Clearing away years of clutter and organizing the shop was no easy task. But PTSD requires therapy, and I'm ready to start workin' on it.

As the foamy soap lathers in my hands, a sharp burning sensation jolts through my skin, sending shockwaves of pain through my body. I yelp. Acid is searing my hands, and the burning is moving to my chest.

Thump.

The soap bottle falls into the sink.

My heart races and a wave of dizziness washes over me, disorienting me and making me rock back on my heels.

Am I having a flashback? A heart attack?

"Paul, you alright?" My pop's concerned voice pierces the haze as he hurries toward me.

I try opening my mouth to assure him everything's okay, but my throat is closed, and only a strained wheeze escapes.

The realization hits me like a freight train—*I'm having an allergic reaction.* To make matters worse, I know where my EpiPen is—*my jacket on my bedroom floor.* Nowhere nearby.

Dammit!

I struggle to stay on my feet, gripping the sink's edge. The world around me blurs as my vision fades to black.

I hear my pop's urgent instructions for my mom to call for an ambulance.

My mom barks orders at Dad to check my pockets for the EpiPen while telling 9-1-1 the situation.

I focus on my dad's voice, speaking a steady mantra. "It's alright. It's alright. It's alright." A reassuring chant and my focal point.

My arms are numb, and I release the sink, collapsing to the floor. My vision is only a tiny tunnel of black narrowing until *nothing.*

The last sound I register is the loud *thwack* of my head bouncing on the concrete floor.

Lucky for me, I've got a skull as thick as a bunker door, is my last thought.

Chapter 12

Mak

Room fourteen is alarming. I rush, ready to calm an escalating patient. The ER's chaos surrounds me - a storm of medical expertise, compassion, and urgency. Amid this, Respiratory Therapist Bryant stands out, a familiar figure in the whirlwind.

"Nice to see you, Bryant," Dr. Anderson says, the ER doctor in charge. His welcoming words skip past me to acknowledge the other male in the room, Bryant.

To be fair, Bryant is an essential and experienced Code Team member, navigating the room's frenetic energy effortlessly and assessing as he pulls out the respiratory supplies. As the Code Team arrives, they flash smiles and nod greetings to him. He's charismatic, and his smile is inviting, even during an emergency. His casual confidence eases the room's heavy atmosphere.

I bite my lip. *If only I had a sliver of love—of desire—for this modern-day Don Juan.* His confidence, easy smile, and intelligence *should* be a perfect match for me.

Watching him work, a complicated tangle of emotions surges within me - a mix of exasperation and longing. His magnetic personality draws others, but I'm more hypnotized by the smooth moves of his hands administering treatments and swiftly moving the patient into position.

"Extra towel," he says.

I hand him a rolled towel to place under the patient's head to hold the position, keeping the airway open. Working alongside him, I predict his moves, making it look like we are a flawless team- the perfect couple-working smoothly side-by-side.

He winks at me and tucks the towel under the patient's neck.

I look away and glance around for the family to comfort, but there are only the patient and staff members in the room.

Does he know about the rumor circulating? How will I get him alone to discuss my new feelings and kibosh our relationship once and for all?

Dr. Anderson nods, approving the tenuous airway placement by Bryant, and looks over to the oxygen monitor.

No. He must not have heard the rumor, or he'd have told me, and he wouldn't be winking at me. Bryant may look like a playboy, but he's honest, making me feel horrible about what I must do today.

I must kick him out and tell him, unlike our previous breakups where we argue and then get back together-*this time is for real!*

I catch a nursing student slowly moving her eyes from his wavy brown hair to his thick biceps and then to his tight butt. At least the nurses' with their sticky eyes and sly smiles, will be excited to hear he is back on the market.

Why can't he move on to find an adoring woman charmed by his humor and Henry Cavill-like handsomeness?

Strangely, the idea of him with this nursing student or anyone else doesn't bother me or make me jealous. It would make this break-up easier, and he deserves passionate love-the kind of love I've discovered.

I blush and join the team, focusing entirely on stabilizing the seizing patient, who seems to have settled. Bryant's expertise and the teams' early interventions have stabilized the patient without any more danger.

I take a breath, and we high-five each other, dispersing as the patient wakes up and all his vital signs are stable.

"Thanks, guys," the nurse, along with the nursing student, says as we leave the room to return to our regular duties.

I need to finish my charting.

"Hey, Mak Attack. I thought you'd call me yesterday. The least you could do is wish me Merry Christmas," Bryant says, catching me in the hallway.

I should have called him, but he should also stop treating our relationship like it's a real relationship.

Turning to face him, our coworkers buzz around us, and I can't say what I need to in this too-public hallway. Instead, I look down the hallway and cross my arms.

The other nurses unwittingly block my path with the code cart and trap me in the hallway with him. Seeing Bryant at work is unavoidable, though, and I need to talk to him when we don't have an audience.

"I was busy," I reply curtly, maneuvering around the cart.

I'll remain professional until we can talk. There's no need to add any validity to the current rumor until we decide how to announce our breakup and cancel our wedding.

He smiles warmly and hands me a mini candy cane from his pocket.

Damn him! Why can't he be an asshole then I'd feel better about our breakup?

"It goes both ways. You could've called me." But I bite my lip, remembering *he did call me,* and I didn't return any of the messages.

I'm the jerk, and he's the good guy.

He shrugs good-naturedly and hands out candy to the passing nurses, who are more enthusiastic than me to receive his attention.

"You're the best, Bry," a nurse purrs at him with a flutter of lashes as she pockets the candy.

I'm terrible at faking or lying, and with an adoring audience around, the pressure is on me to keep my interactions with him normal until we talk. I look at the clock. Only a few more hours, then my shift is done, and I can discuss the whole situation with him and home so we can make a game plan that might save my job and not make me look like such a jerk for canceling the wedding.

Ignoring the nurse's flirting, Bryant follows me. His demeanor shifts, and he leans in, his words loaded with familiarity, and whispers, "Hey, you know I've been thinking about us."

He hands another candy cane to the nursing student, who has no reason to hang out in the hallway. He winks at her and then grabs my hand to stop my escape.

Meeting his gaze cautiously, I respond firmly and shake my hand out of his grip. I'm tired of this recurring conversation.

"Bryant, we've been through this. We're better off apart, and you can literally have any nurse here. You promised you'd move out over the holidays and we would talk to HR together and announce our breakup."

His smile fades at my calm response. And his eyes flash, the warmth replaced by a sudden intensity. "You aren't giving me a chance, Mak. We've been together too long to break up suddenly. At least give me another shot. I am going to be on the mortgage, and you were just starting to combine our accounts, so I can take care of all our financial stuff, while you take care of the household and our kids."

Kids! Am I hallucinating?

I give a shake and look into his eyes. *I wish I felt as committed to him and our future as he feels about me.* It's Christmas, and he's ending a long-term relationship which is difficult. He's probably a little blue and lonely this holiday.

He's right. *I should have called him.*

"No," I say, firmer this time. I won't give in to his attempts to rekindle our relationship or let him believe we have a future.

I quickly scan the hall, silently praying for Jessica to rescue me, but I only see other staff milling about.

No luck.

"You tell patients to be open-minded in trying new therapies." His words hang in the air.

Guilt creeps into my heart, making me want to give in to him. I know prolonging our relationship and breakup isn't good for us. But he's really hurt, and everyone deserves a second chance.

I shake my head. We've rehashed this conversation too many times for me to do it one more time.

He leans closer, his eyes searching. "Mak Attack , remember all the good times we've had. The plans we made. The life we have together. You can't just throw all of it away."

I sigh and rub my forehead. "Bryant, the past is the past. We've *both* changed, and it's time to move on."

His voice softens, and he reaches for my hand, but I stuff it into my lab coat's pocket.

"I love you, Mak. I have since I first saw you and Jess introduced us. Give me one more chance, for old times' sake. *Please.*"

I meet his gaze, my eyes unwavering. "Bryant, love isn't enough. We need more than history to make this work. I'm not happy and you aren't happy. It's time we *both* find happiness elsewhere."

He opens his mouth to protest, but I don't give him a chance to continue. I turn away, determined to end this no-win conversation.

We still share a house and a workplace. *I must maintain civility.* I agreed to let him be the one to announce the breakup after he moved out and to stay on friendly terms with him since we must work together. But I'm unsure what he will do when he finds out I met someone else.

"You'll never find a guy who's willing to be in a relationship with all your baggage. Plus, I could have any woman I want. Do you see the way the nurses' look at me? You're making a big mistake," he mutters in a low tone, keeping our conversation discreet.

His spiteful words, intended to make me apologize, have the opposite effect.

I smile. "Bryant, you're right. But then you're always right, aren't you?" My agreement disarms him.

He smiles triumphantly, done arguing with me, and extends his hand for me to take it as if it only took him mansplaining the situation to make me want to stay with him.

I lean forward to whisper, "You're right. I won't find another *guy* like you because I don't *want to be with you.* I'm in love with someone else." I slide off my mom's ring and put it in my pocket. I don't want him to misconstrue that I'm wearing the ring because of him and not to honor my mother.

I'm done with trying to save my job, make him look good, and pretend to be someone I'm not. I can't do it, and it's not fair to Bryant!

His hand clenches into a fist, and his face contorts with the rage of a man scorned, *which he is.*

"Mak, I'll tell HR that I'm unwilling to work with you and you'll get fired. I'll tell everyone you're a cheating *slut* and make sure you can't move to another department," he spews, his words stinging like a slap. "You'll give me another chance *or else*. I haven't wasted a year of my life *for nothing*."

Before I react, the intercom diverts our attention.

"CODE BLUE ER 4. CODE BLUE ER 4!"

His intensity wavers, replaced by the profession in him. It's as if nothing happened, and he conveniently forgets the threat to me as he pivots to room four. His intense, threatening demeanor dissolves, replaced by the confidence he effortlessly wears. In the blink of an eye, he's an ER team member, focused on the task.

I move with the flow of our coworkers, their attention fixed on the impending crisis, unaware of the tense undercurrent.

Chapter 13

Mak

I settle into my chair to complete the final round of charting for the day. Exhausted and drained, I chart on my patient, who is close to alcohol poisoning because of her holiday family stress. The radio crackles with the EMTs calling from the helicopter, jolting me out of my weariness. An emergency patient is coming to us.

I multitask, trying to type up my notes double-quick and wishing I could get a coffee, but I don't have time to pee anyway.

I should've known better than to work on Christmas—*It's a full moon! Codes are being called every few minutes. I'm fighting with Bryant!*

In the background, the EMT's brief report crackles over the radio to prepare us for the emergency transfer en route.

"Ninilchik... a twenty-five-year-old woman, in respiratory distress ... possible anaphylactic reaction ... eighteen-gauge IV placement ... unknown history ..."

My heart flutters with anxiety, and my thoughts suddenly drift to Paul—probably because Paul is dominating my thoughts all shift. *He's twenty-five-ish from Ninilchik.* I shake the idea from my head, trying to finish charting, and ignore the radio.

It's a coincidence. I bite my bottom lip and taste salt.

What if this is Paul?

Ninilchik is full of people—I'm sure my one-night stand isn't the patient being rushed here. Even with a full moon, this is too far-fetched. My overthinking and nerves are getting the best of me.

My stomach clenches, and my hand covers the medallion at my throat. *God, tell me I'm wrong, and give me strength if I'm not.*

Even if it is Paul—an improbable *scenario*-an anaphylactic reaction is easily fixed. I can handle seeing him, and there's no shame as it wasn't some lewd, illicit affair. *I'm a single adult, after all.*

Love isn't bound by gender expectations nowadays, right? The hospital doesn't need to know, and they are *supposedly* becoming *more progressive.*

I must be tired or hungry. Or tired *and* hungry because why does my brain jump to *worst-case scenarios?*

Also, *two people in a blizzard, alone in the wilderness-a hook-up would've happened to anyone in that situation, according to every romance story ever written.*

The picture of Jesus hanging by the clock *judges me* and disagrees.

Oh God, please, please don't let this be Paul!

The backdoor slams open, and I shut the chart to greet the patient as the EMTs push into the ER. Machines and people surround the gurney, but I notice a Santa hat with green glitter tucked into the pile of belongings at the foot of the bed.

My hat! Paul!

My heart lurches in my chest, and I gasp. My professionalism unravels. Tears unwittingly pool in my eyes, and I clutch my Saint Michael, whispering a prayer for protection as my eyes water.

Paul is buried in blankets, an oxygen mask covering his face, and tubes and wires weaving around him. He looks vulnerable yet captivating, an embodiment of raw strength, the inked arms with ropy muscles and the pale fragility intersecting. The machines dwarf his powerful frame, but there's no doubt—this strong person who rescued me in the blizzard last night and carried me to safety in those IV-laced arms.

My professional demeanor crumbles, and I cannot stop my emotional response. Instinct takes over as I rush to Paul's side. Instead of taking the chart or helping to push the gurney, I reach my trembling hand to touch him.

I want to assure this is real and reassure him that I'm here and he's okay.

A tender murmur is on my lips as he grimaces and tenses with the EMTs, bumping him through the doorway. I ache to wrap Paul in my arms and transfer my strength to his fragile body.

Reality stops me, and I stop moving, making me stand awkwardly in the hallway. I can't embrace Paul in a room full of my colleagues and the prying eyes of my ex. Besides, Paul might not even have the same feelings for me. *It was one crazy night.*

My heart pounds, an increasing drumbeat thundering in my ears as I stand torn between professionalism and the tumultuous emotions surging inside me. I've got to keep it together and remain composed. But that's easier said than done.

Rather than comfort him, I open the emergency room five's door, my fingers trembling slightly as I pull the curtains aside, revealing the sterile interior of the trauma room.

Jessica is taking charge of the room with the monitors set up and ready to transfer the patient to the bed. Her eyes flick toward me with an unspoken question.

"Do you know her?" she inquires, her eyebrows raised as the EMTs heave Paul onto our bed.

I lock eyes with her and bite my lip. Words fail, and I chew inside my cheeks, unable to articulate the emotions threatening to spill out.

A nod from Jessica tells me she notices my tears, and she moves the patient's belongings to the table, pulling out my hat to sit on top of the pile. She looks at me, her eyes widen as she understands and is putting together the pieces from my odd admission of falling in love, the Bryant rumor, and Paul appearing in our Emergency Department from Ninilchik with my hat.

Her eyes hold unasked questions—*What is going on?*—but there's no time for answers right now.

Paul's difficult breathing fills the room, a whistling, high-pitched inhalation jolting us into action.

My feet are encased in cement, rooting me to the ground as I watch, helpless.

He's groggy, his skin an alarming shade of blue, and each of his desperate gasps are a knife wounding my heart. I hold my throat and do the only thing I can think of—*pray.*

"We need to intubate her ASAP. We're losing her airway," Jessica says, cutting through the chaos.

Brant pushes me aside. "Move, Mak," he says, irritated, as he moves equipment beside Paul, the situation's urgency prompting him to action.

I want to stay by his side and offer comfort, but simultaneously, I realize *I need to leave*—immediately.

"Mak, is she a full code? Any medical history?" Jess's questions pierce through my fog, demanding answers.

Bryant looks at Jessica, spots the Santa hat, and then looks at me, his eyes narrowing.

A breath escapes my lips, and I force myself to respond, my voice steady despite my heart hammering. "Full code. Give him everything," I reply.

"Let's get the airway secure," Dr. Anderson orders.

In a swift and fluid motion, the emergency technician swiftly peels away Paul's shirt, exposing the chest binder splayed open beneath him. At the same time, the relentless glare of the hospital lights illuminates this intimate intrusion. A gasp escapes my lips as I witness his private, vulnerable form violated in this sterile environment. Tracing down his arms, the scars I kissed intertwine with his military tattoos, hinting at his traumatic past.

Paul, breathe!

"He's an army veteran, dealing with PTSD, but otherwise in good health," I say, recalling snippets of our conversation last night.

"He?" Bryant scoffs as he positions Paul's oxygen mask.

"Do we have another respiratory therapist for this patient?" I hear Jessica whisper to a nurse. The nurse leaves, hopefully calling in another RT to replace Bryant.

"Yes, Paul is *trans* and uses the pronoun *He*. If you have a problem with that, you should get out!" I snap, pointing to the door.

Dr. Anderson looks up for a beat but says nothing, focused on his stethoscope over Paul's lungs.

The ER tech gasps, and Bryant's jaw tightens at my outburst, but the medical team continues working as if staff arguments are routine. Jessica shoots me a reassuring nod as she focuses on Paul's needs, deftly removing the binder from under him while moving the blanket to maintain his dignity and privacy.

Thank God Jessica's here!

I look away from Bryant's acidic stare, and Paul struggles to breathe. The person I spent an unforgettable night with is here. Fear, love, regret, and longing propel through me with every woosh of my heart.

As the team continues to work, I'm left standing in the doorway, torn between my professional duty of detachment and my emotions swelling. My St. Michael's medallion is cool and reassuring under my fingertips as I watch. As the team continues, I'm paralyzed in the threshold, caught between my obligation of detachment and the surging tides of my fervent sentiments. The medallion against my skin grants a resolute chill that steadies me as I pray, watching the scene.

"Do you know his allergies?" the doctor asks.

Bryant's face contorts into a deep scowl as I falter, my recollection shrouded in a fog of uncertainty and my thoughts spiraling frantically.

"Umm...He carries an EpiPen and is allergic to lavender and ginger," I add, trying to remember the information Paul told me when I woke him to his EpiPen falling from his pocket.

"Medications?"

"No ... Well. Maybe," I hesitate. With my mind racing, I can't grasp the answer.

I wish I could remember more.

"Get outta the way already so we can work on her," Bryant yells from across the room at me.

He's rude but right.

I am hindering instead of aiding. As my gaze meets Jessica's, her expression changes to grave, with her lips tight and her eyes on Paul. She'll ensure Paul receives the necessary care, leaving me no choice but to retreat from the room.

Outside, I snap into action. I will notify Paul's family and update them on his condition. Also, since he's military, I'll call the Veterans Hospital and get his records *stat.*

Jessica passed by me, grabbing more intravenous fluids, an epinephrine vial, and Benadryl from the medication cart. I watch from the nurses' station, determined not to interfere or ask how Paul's doing.

She needs to focus, and I don't want to delay his care.

As she swings open the door to the trauma bay, a sinister wheezing escapes from Paul's unconscious form. The urgency intensifies as they struggle to secure his airway, with every passing moment becoming more critical.

My hand instinctively reaches for my throat, feeling the weight of impending doom. If the wheezing and swelling persist, Paul will be in trouble soon! A whirlwind of thoughts swirls through my mind as I desperately search for the fragments of knowledge teasing me.

God, what am I forgetting?

"Get me another vial of Benadryl!" Dr Anderson shouts, and I blindly grab the vial from the nursing station cart and follow the shouts back into Paul's room.

As I hand the medication to Dr. Anderson, Bryant's voice pulls me from my coursing thoughts.

"So you know her, huh?"

He's adeptly pulling out the nebulizer and breathing medications to administer to Paul.

"I do, and as I said earlier, *Paul's a him, not a her*," I reply simply, my emotions boiling beneath the surface.

"How?" His inquiry is a loaded question, and I note his hands in fists and his searing gaze.

"None of your business," I snap back, irritation making my voice louder.

His attention should be fully on Paul's breathing, not on me.

Our gazes lock in a silent but deafening argument. If my coworkers doubted the break-up rumor, there's no question of its truth seeing us now. Bryant's jaw is tight, and his eyes are hard with hurt and anger.

"What do you think, Doctor? Does the army tranny need to be tubed to breathe?" he asks, looking directly at me and not Dr Anderson.

"His name is Paul!" I say in a rush, and Jessica grabs my suddenly raised-fisted hand.

Bryant snatches the chest binder forcefully from the table, launching it toward me with a fiery fury. "Get out and find a different boyfriend to cheat on!"

I manage to catch the binder mid-air, clutching it tightly against my quivering body, desperate to quell the anger coursing through me.

Dr. Anderson steps to the head of the bed between Bryant and me. "Let's watch Paul," he says, using his preferred gender, "seems to be improving with the breathing treatment. Keep the intubation breathing kit at the bedside."

Jessica nods, and the requested new Respiratory Therapist appears.

"Gina, take over for Bryant. *He's on break.*" Jessica meets my eyes and releases my hand to dismiss me, too.

Bryant steps back, handing the breathing nebulizer machine to Gina.

I flash a quick smile, my fingers gripping the binder tightly and then setting it down. Jess's nod tells me she's in control and will protect Paul.

As Bryant inches closer to me while making his departure, there is an unnerving proximity that sends shivers down my spine.

His eyebrows raise as he growls with an air of astonishment. "Paul? Really? That's a unique name for a lady," he remarks, his tone dripping with incredulity.

Suppressing my mounting irritation, I respond with a forced smile that barely conceals my simmering fury. "Unique? Paul is the perfect name for him," I retort sharply, the words laced with venomous defiance and unwavering resolve.

He says, "So *Paul's* the cock blocker, huh? I expected a burly Alaskan man. Guess I misread you."

"Completely," I agree, glaring back. My cheeks are red, and my hands form fists again.

I focus back on Paul's monitor from the hallway and am relieved to see the numbers improving.

"A woman. Really? You're no lesbo," he mutters.

I tilt my head and ignore Bryant and the stares from our coworkers. *The rumor mill is going to be churning tonight!*

"We can laugh this off at home. Why don't you let me show you what being with a man is like? Then you'll stop this nonsense," he says in a lower tone, forgetting the audience.

In the tense moment, Jessica's eyes darted to me, overhearing his growls. She scans us to see if I need backup.

I mouth, *I'm okay*. I'll explain this messy situation to Jess after she stabilizes Paul and we are off-shift.

For now, her unwavering attention is on Paul and his dwindling oxygen levels. She may be my friend, but she is a nurse first and will do anything to protect her patient, including kicking Bryant and me out of the room.

I save her the worry and move to the nurses' station with Bryant trailing me.

"It's not what you think—" I say, but it *kinda is*. Then I take a breath and look at him squarely. "I told you we are done, and it's nothing to do with you. *I love Paul, and I don't love you."*

As my words hang heavy between us, I watch anger and hurt flash across his eyes. His usually confident gaze falters, replaced by a fiery intensity. His pupils narrow, sharpening into daggers, his brows furrowing as he contains his seething anger.

He smiles, remembering the audience, and talks to me and the onlooking staff at the nurses' station. "Do tell, Mak Attack. Even better, show us the pictures," he laughs, his eyes daggers.

"Stop, Bryant," I hiss. "We have a patient to take care of."

Before he presses any further, Jessica calls out, "Did we get the chart from the VA?"

I take a deep breath and turn away from his cutting gaze to check the fax machine. "I'll see."

The nurses' desk buzzes with activity as my heart races with anxiety at the dangerous situation and the scene Bryant is causing.

I pull papers from the fax, and one piece of information grabs my attention, leaping off the page: *Benadryl allergy.*

In the cabin, amidst our intimate conversations, Paul divulged all his secrets, including this one. This crucial detail slipped through the cracks of my memory and now thunders in my mind.

Panic courses through my veins as I sprint back to Paul's room. The sound of his labored breaths is worse and amplified by the confining mask and his silent, unconscious form.

"Benadryl!" I exclaim urgently, the word tumbling out of my mouth. "Paul is allergic to Benadryl."

Without hesitation, Jessica clamps the IV Benadryl drip shut and exchanges it for a saline bag to flush it out of the system, moving with practiced precision.

The doctor nods. "Good catch, Doctor Jackson. He was starting to decompensate again, heading back into respiratory distress."

Thank God for small miracles. I touch St. Michael and look at Paul's monitor, showing his heart and breathing slowing to a regular rate.

"Excellent work, everyone," the doctor's voice rings out, a proclamation signifying the end of the emergency.

We can stand down.

As Paul rests, his breathing steady and no longer in distress, I take a deep breath and glance out the window. The moon bathes the snow-covered city in a gentle, ethereal glow. I look back to Paul.

Another snowy night with an emergency, and this time, I saved you!

As emotions engulf me, an overwhelming surge of relief swells, threatening to burst through my calm exterior. Tears cascade down my cheeks, acting as a release valve for the immense weight of tension that I've been carrying since Paul came into the ER. With bated breath, the medical team silently retreats from the room, leaving behind a flickering monitor and Jessica attentively watching Paul.

Jess nods and brushes by me, gently touching my arm as she leaves the bedside since Paul is stable and resting.

I break my gaze from Paul.

"Good job, Mak. You stay here and I'll let you know if you're needed. You only have an hour left on your shift anyways and I think Paul would appreciate you here."

I numbly nod and take the seat by Paul.

She shuts the curtains behind herself, leaving us alone.

With the calmer atmosphere, Paul stirs, his eyes fluttering open. My eyes meet his, and his sleepy eyes reflect recognition and warmth. He hasn't forgotten our unspoken connection from last night.

Paul's fingers twitch, and his hand reaches out for mine.

I grasp his hand, and he smiles, drifting back to sleep with the steady beat of the monitors and my hand warming his.

"Merry Christmas, Paul," I whisper, kissing his hand.

Chapter 14

Mak

"Paul," my voice trembles as I clasp his hand, "There's something I need to confess. Something I've realized but I didn't tell you."

We are alone as the morning sun dances upon the frost-kissed windowpane, casting icy sparkles throughout the room. My Christmas night shift ended hours ago, but I remained at Paul's bedside, unable to leave. As I watch Paul in this hospital room, our fleeting connection has grown into an unexpectedly intimate bond.

God keeps bringing us together for a reason.

The soft, rhythmic beeping of the heart monitor and Paul's breaths are within normal ranges. Reason tells me his survival is assured, but my heart refuses to accept such certainties. I can't bear to leave Paul's side if there's a chance he could go into respiratory distress and need me to rescue him again.

Bryant and my coworkers have an inkling of my innermost feelings, yet there's one person to whom I concealed the depths of my emotions. The thought of baring my heart to Paul fills me with unease as if by saying aloud, I will ruin our connection. Deep down, I know I should've told my truth at the cabin. Yet I ignored it and said nothing when I had the chance.

With my feelings haunting me ever since waking up with Paul on Christmas Eve, I don't plan to ignore it this time. *What if something had happened to Paul and he didn't wake up?*

I'm telling Paul and everyone else, too.

Paul's chest rises and falls with the steady rhythm of slumber, a reassuring movement. I gather strength from him, knowing he's here with me. Even if he doesn't hear me, I need to tell him.

I start, "I knew I was different, and conventional relationships never quite fit." I continue, my words heavy with the weight of memories. "I had my life planned out, as a doctor, then a big wedding, thinking I knew my path. But God's will or *fate*, if you'd rather call it that, has a funny way of surprising me."

Inhaling deeply, I feel my heart pounding as I struggle to tell Paul. "I've fallen in love with you, Paul," I confess in a whisper. "And you're not at all part of my plan."

Tears blur my vision as I explain my truth, which I can no longer deny, even if it costs me my job.

"I never imagined I could feel this way for someone. Loving you is so natural and easy," I say, trembling. "I finally understand why I couldn't fall in love with Bryant and why I couldn't initiate a physical relationship with him. He wasn't the right person."

Paul stirs in their sleep, a soft murmur escaping his lips, urging me to continue telling him my secrets, similar to how he whispered his secrets to me. I grasp Paul's hands, and a smile plays on his lips.

"I ended the engagement before I met you but without properly explaining the reasons to him. And he couldn't move on because I didn't even understand why I didn't-*couldn't*- love him. *Not until I met you*," I stroke Paul's cheek lightly.

"Bryant," I whisper, my grip on Paul's hand tightening, "my ex-fiancé, didn't truly love me. He loved the idea of being engaged to a doctor, and of having me as a status symbol on his arm. And he wasn't a terrible person. There's this pressure from my parents, then my coworkers, and after my parents died, I didn't want to change everything they were so proud of me for. I've been lying to my friends and coworkers—And *lying to myself about who I am*."

Tears stream down my cheeks as I bare my soul, each word a cathartic release.

"It didn't *feel* like such a terrible lie, only a *little* lie. And I was going to tell everyone the truth after Bryant moved out. Then I met *you*," I say, pausing to look at Paul's relaxed and radiant face. "You helped me discover real love and passion and *who I am*. Now my little lie feels like a *huge* deception that spilled out, and I can't keep hiding it."

Paul sleeps peacefully.

I continue, "I trapped myself in this false relationship and false narrative. I didn't fully understand that I didn't love Bryant. Working in a Catholic hospital and having traditional parents, I didn't consider a different path. The truth is, *I did know*, deep in my heart, and you gave me the strength to confront it."

I take another deep breath and place my hand on my medallion to gather strength from the St Michael medallion, like the one my father wore.

A lightness washes over me, and I hold Paul's hand. "When you arrived by EMT, and I saw you on the gurney, I realized I made a mistake. I needed to tell you how I feel, what you mean to me. I should have told you yesterday at the cabin."

"You fill my heart and love me for who I am. I have to tell you," I confess, my heart beating faster as I speak aloud, "I love you, Paul. That's it. *I love you.*"

The truth is out, and I'm free of my secret. *I only hope Paul feels the same.*

A throat clearing surprises me, and Jessica is standing in the doorway. Her eyes are unblinking, but she's smiling.

I wipe my moist eyes and offer a shrug. "I'm sorry, Jess. I guess I'm not exactly who you thought I was."

Her radiant smile reaches her eyes, and her eyes twinkle at me. "You're a wonderful doctor and friend, which is exactly who I know you are. I don't care who your partner is and I didn't want to wear an ugly bridesmaid dress anyways. I want you to be *you* and happy."

Our eyes meet, understanding passing between us, and her friendship makes me smile warmly back to her.

She tilts her head toward the door and then closes it—the mood shifts. "Bryant was up at HR this morning, looking very smug, and I don't like it," she confides in a low voice as she clasps her hands together.

I frown. I thought-*hoped*- Bryant went home to pack and move out once and for all.

"Whatever happens, me and the rest of the staff have your back, Mak. You deserve to be here as much as any other doctor or respiratory therapist. This hospital's Catholic old-fashioned morality clauses are ridiculous."

Chapter 15

Paul

My eyelids blink open reluctantly, and the sterile scent of antiseptic, white walls, and the rhythmic beeping of monitors greet me. A flickering fluorescent light overhead amplifies the throbbing, jagged pain in my head. I squeeze them shut again.

Hospital.

I'm in the damn hospital, waking up just like after my army platoon's attack. A painful lightning bolt hits from my temple to the base of my skull.

My thoughts are foggy, but my brain recalibrates to the present as the throbbing subsides. *I'm not in the army.*

The accident at the shop, my parents, the Emergency Room, and Mak's voice, the whole ordeal floods into my head in broken bits and pieces. I move my hands to my head, expecting to feel a dent, like a car's busted fender after hitting a snowbank. There's a bandage, but it's intact despite the throbbing.

Clearer thoughts filter back into my consciousness. *Mak.*

Mak was here. She held my hand and whispered in my ear. She was at my bedside.

I force my eyes to stay open, shifting my gaze to the side of my bed. Sitting in the chair next to me isn't Mak. Instead, a stranger stares quietly, intensely at me.

My heart rate ratchets up, and I clench my fists ready.

He doesn't react and sits unmoving, studying me with an unsettling gaze. I'm his prey through the sniper's scope, and his calm, explosive stare denotes danger.

What is he planning? Who is he?

Lightning strikes my temple again, and I grimace, which makes him stand.

He's young, fit, with no visible weapons, wearing blue scrubs and a nametag pinned to his pocket.

"Bryant," I croak out with a gravelly voice.

He doesn't respond and maintains his unsettling stare, sizing me up from the dominant attack position above me. *He's hostile as hell.*

I fist my hand around the heavy call light to pack more of a punch.

Breaking eye contact with me, he lifts his chin at a vase of pink carnations sitting by the window.

I squint, keeping him within my sight as I try to make sense of the man and flowers in my room. *He didn't bring the flowers, and I didn't buy them.* Plus, I have no friends, and my parents would've got me a burger, not flowers.

The thought of my parents makes me break eye contact with the enemy, scanning the room again. My heart pounds louder than my head. My mind races, and it clicks.

Pretty, pink, casual flowers—*Mak.*

"Those are Mak Attack's favorite, too," he says, biting each word.

Suddenly, the pieces click into place, and the gears in my brain turn. *Mak must've left them here while I was sleeping—a token since she had to work, or she wasn't ready to out herself with me at work.*

I'm trying to remember anything she whispered, but only her warm presence remains. My banged-up brain missed the exact words or where she said she was going.

I lick my dry lips and manage a weak hacking cough before grunting, "You doin' a test or something?"

"Your breathing's fine, thanks to me." His tone remains cool, eerily flat.

I narrow my eyes, his arrogant posturing grating on my nerves. I've stayed in hospitals long enough to know it's *a team,* not one person that takes care of a patient. If anyone is to thank, my heart tells me it's Mak.

"Yeah," I mutter, my headache pounding as my heart rate slows, making speaking difficult, but I am ready for the fight.

His smirk falters, an icy stare replacing it. "Don't get any ideas, *Pauline.* Mak's mine and marrying me. She's *not gay.*"

He spits out the last part, and I unclench my fist, releasing the call light. He won't fight me-he's a chained dog, barking. This must be who gave her that ring.

"Her parents would turn over in their graves at *you.* They raised her to be a good Catholic girl, for God's sake! She doesn't know what she wants and needs someone to take care of her."

His words reek of possessiveness, and anger surges through me instead of fear.

Does this guy think he can claim Mak? Like hell he can! She's a grown-ass woman, not anyone's property, and I won't let this jerk stomp her down.

I lift my chin, my intensity meeting his gaze. With clipped words, I say, "Mak's choices are hers. She's more than capable of picking *who* she wants to be with."

His eyes spark, and his lips curl into a sardonic smile. He towers over my bed, relishing his position. "Right. *Doctor* Mak makes great life choices: driving into a winter storm without snow tires or chains. She was asking for me to spend the holiday with her. She wanted me to chase her and save her. That's not a capable, intelligent woman, is it? She wants *a man to* take care of her."

My fists clenched, my patience wearing thin at his impotent conversation. *I need sleep.* "What's your problem?"

He moves in further, his breath attacking. "My problem? You shouldn't have been out there. I had everything under control. I would've saved her, and you almost got her killed."

His words ignite my fuse, amplifying the painful throbbing. *Who does this guy think he is?* Mak doesn't need this asshat stalking her.

"Mak can handle herself. You can leave," I growl at him, my pain adding a fierceness to my words.

"Oh, really? Are *you* going to save her? You're a real *lesbo in shining armor*, I see," he sneers.

Narrowing my eyes and pushing through the throbbing pain, I say, "You don't know a damn thing about *either* of us."

Tension fills the room, and I wait for the explosion. My heart rate ratchets upwards. I glance around, half-expecting my platoon at my back, a show of force. But it's the two of us, no witnesses.

He should be afraid. I'm in control and won't *allow* this asshat to belittle Mak and threaten me.

"*Miss Pauline*," he taunts, saying my unused legal name, "You are really messing up my plans." His tone drips with arrogance. He steps from my bedside, backs down, and pokes around my room.

I keep my eyes glued on him and the door, wrapping my hand around the call light, ready for his approach.

"Leave Mak alone. Her parents died, and she's emotional and confused. She's nothing like you and she's my fiancé."

He pummels my chest binder at me like a grenade, and I flinch.

I leave it on my bed, my focus remaining on him as I wait, prepared.

"Or else," I challenge. I'm in no condition to fight, my lungs burning, my head splitting, but I'm a trained soldier. My body is tense with the threat of this inflated man-child.

Newsflash: he couldn't win a fight against me even if I had no arms.

I wait for his response, wondering how much trouble I'll get into for punching a hospital employee. It probably won't be much, but I don't want to add stress to Mak's plate.

He leans back, his demeanor shifting from threatening to amusement. "Oh, you don't know, *do you?* About *her* and *me?*"

A foreboding tightens in my chest. "What?"

His eyes narrow as he puffs his chest out, smugly saying, "She came back and begged me to stay with her. She wants a big wedding and to have my children. We *live* together, and she's not leaving me. She's Catholic, if anyone finds out about you then she loses everything. She's not destroying her career and her life for *a freak*."

His words hit me like a sledgehammer, a cocktail of disbelief and betrayal coursing through my veins. My head aches, struggling to process.

Mak and he are living together?

My muddled brain can't sort fact from fiction. Bryant is handsome, and if Mak has to pick between a doctor and a fucked-up army vet, I'm not sure she'd pick me, especially if her career is involved.

Whispers of last night's conversation start resurfacing, and I'm sure she told me she cared for me. *Didn't she, or did I imagine it?*

The lightning in my head vies with the anger exploding in my gut. Bryant's words pound in the harsh truth of Mak's decision, and the lightning in my head adds to my defeat. His smug demeanor fuels my need to fight, though.

"You're a lying piece of shit," I spit, my voice cracking. I knew my dream-*Mak*—was too good to be true.

He leans in, his eyes reflecting the twisted satisfaction of winning. "Am I? Think about it, *Paulinah*. Do you honestly believe she'd choose a broken lesbo soldier over *me?*"

"You're a lying shit," I repeat, my voice more potent this time, despite the throbbing in my head. I will not let Bryant break me.

"Mak and I share something special. Something she never had with you."

Bryant's face contorts with a blend of anger and frustration. Clearly, he didn't expect me to stand up to him and his threats.

"Did you sleep with her?" His face turns bright red, and he faces me with his fists.

I stare him down without acknowledging anything but the deadly force I will use.

"You don't know her," he snaps. "She needs stability, her job here, not some wild, meaningless fling with a mentally unstable soldier."

"She might not pick me," I say, "But she's not going to pick an *asshole, like you*!"

His face darkens, his eyes narrow, locking onto mine, and the room crackles with the anger between us.

"You have no idea what I went through with her. How much *she* owes me," he hisses. "I put in the time and dealt with her backward *good Catholic girl beliefs of saving herself for her husband—Me!*"

My fingers clenched into fists beneath the hospital sheets. "Mak's capable of making her own choice. And if she chose you -*unlikely*-I'll respect that. But trying to force her and sayin' *she owes you*—that's not love, bro."

My door swings open, and a nurse comes to an abrupt halt, seeing us. She looks behind herself and at me as if she's entered the wrong room. Then she steps forward.

"Is everything alright here?" Her gaze shifts to Bryant. "What are you doing, Bryant?"

He straightens up, irritation coloring his tone. "Hey, Jessica. We're just having a conversation."

"You can't *be* here. Another respiratory therapist is assigned to him." She moves closer and points to the door for emphasis.

Instead of moving, he takes a menacing step closer to me, his body rigid.

As she takes another step forward, Jessica's demeanor indicates she can handle a threat and a fight if needed. "Bryant, I *understand* the situation. *Get. Out. Now.*"

He flushes. "You don't know anything!"

She moves closer and maneuvers between Bryant and me. Her tone remains stern, addressing him. "I understand you're a weasel trying to start a fight with someone in a hospital bed and trying to get my friend fired. And now, you want to manipulate her into marrying you. You're pathetic, and I'm sorry I ever introduced her to you. I'm calling a *Code Strong* if you aren't gone in one second."

She moves her hand over the sizable red code button on the wall, and he retreats, huffing.

"Jess, I'm the one who was dumped so don't treat me like the asshole!"

She grabs his arm and practically shoves him from the room. "Good decision. You don't want to lose your job today."

My eyes widen, and I stay wordless at Jessica's actions. *She's Mak's friend.*

Her added information makes the pieces fit. If Jessica knows he's manipulating Mak, then Mak knows.

I hope to God Mak isn't planning on marrying him!

"Where's Mak? Is she going to lose her job?" I ask, my gaze fixed on Mak's friend and my brain spinning as my heartbeat lowers.

"Mak's alright, and you're fine too. She stayed with you all night and went to the lounge to shower for her shift," she assures me.

She looks at the door and clears her throat. "I'm sorry. I wouldn't have left if I knew he was coming in to bother you."

I shrug. At least I figured out why she wore a wedding band, and I've met Mak's fiancé—*ex-fiancé.* "No prob."

"You have visitors, and I can't keep them out any longer." She goes to the door and waves.

My parents enter, and I wonder, *how much of our conversation did they overhear?*

My pop grins, "I'm glad to see you are well enough to give the staff hell."

My mom looks at me and asks, "Did you punch that guy? He looked like he was punched."

"Nah, just makin' friends. You know me," I say, relieved to see them.

The nurse interrupts, "Dr. Anderson mentioned you'll be discharged this afternoon, and your parents can drive you home." She nods and steps back, allowing my parents to surround me.

"Thanks," I mutter.

I wonder if I'll get the chance to see Mak before I leave.

Chapter 16

Mak

The St. Mary's Alaska Emergency Department lies quiet compared to the bustle of yesterday's shift. My fingers curl around my third cup of coffee, its warmth seeping into my palms. I appreciate the caffeine jolt for my sleepy brain and the warm cup on this frosty day.

"Have you talked to Paul yet?" Jessica asks. It's the same question she's asked every hour *as if* I could forget.

"I will. He's sleeping and I'm waiting for *the right time*," I say.

She gives me a you-can't-fool-me look and then asks, "What about Bryant?"

She's relentless. I want to forget about my personal drama and focus on work. Too much is happening too quickly. I'm getting whiplash and need a moment to breathe.

She raises an eyebrow and asks, "Did you happen to see what was in the back of Bryant's truck?"

I pause at the change of topic, taking a sip. *Snow?*

"Jess, I'm done with him. I'm packing and moving *today,* even if it means giving him the house. I can't live under the same roof as him."

"Good." She nods. "You can stay with me. But I wanted to say he's got snow chains in his truck. I'm sure he's going to apologize and give them to you. He cares. Don't get me wrong, he's a transphobic jerk, but he's also Catholic." She shrugs, "You've been together a long time. You could give him one last chance. I mean, are you sure about Paul?"

I contemplated her words, my thoughts swirling like the snow outside the unit's windows. Before I answer her, footsteps approach, making me glance up.

Bryant, with a smirk, strolls past the desk. He must have overheard Jess.

Why did he volunteer to work a double and stay here with me? To win me back or to keep me away from Paul?

The truth hits me with a slap, making me gasp.

He didn't have time to buy me snow chains. Those are my missing chains-he used my spare keys and *removed my Jeep's winter chains before I left to go to the cabin. He sabotaged me!*

"Hey, Mak Attack. I'm really sorry about what I said to Pauline—"

I shoot up from my chair, the force causing it to crash to the floor. *Pauline? Really!*

Jess stands too, uncertain of the situation but standing at my side as my backup.

"How could you?" I direct my anger at him, and he raises his hands, stopping and looking at the growing audience.

I don't give him a chance to respond.

"You hate that Paul rescued me," I say, trembling, "Because you orchestrated the situation to leave me stranded in a blizzard. You took my chains! You tried to kill me!" My words are loud and fill the quiet unit.

"I would've come if you called. It's your fault. Why didn't you call and ask for help like a normal human being? Why would you choose a cabin in the woods for Christmas Eve, anyways? You should've chosen me and been home with me!" He matches my volume, his hands on his hips.

A heavy silence hangs in the air, and the nurses turn to me, waiting to see how I'll respond.

"We aren't together. You aren't my fiancé and you aren't my hero," I continue, "You could've killed me. Did you even think about that?"

The room is charged, and Bryant's face is an angry shade of crimson. "Spare me the sob story, Mak," he says. "You need someone to take care of you and hold your hand, or you make idiotic choices like driving in a blizzard or hooking up with *a freak* to make me jealous."

Jessica steps forward, her hand protectively on my arm, while the ER doctor moves to stand on the other side of me.

"Yes, I didn't choose you. I chose a freak because I'm different too—something you'd realize if you took the time to get to know me instead of using me as your arm candy," I retorted, my hand moving to my neck.

Bryant opens his mouth to respond, but I stop him.

"Paul isn't a freak," I say, my hands moving to my hips and stepping forward. "He is a hero who selflessly served our country and saved my life without hesitation. I'm tired of your toxic attitude and your twisted narrative. I should have stood up to you and told you the truth. I don't love you, and I couldn't because I'm queer! I love Paul."

The room holds its collective breath as the words echo. These words haven't been uttered in this hospital, let alone by a staff member, *ever.* The room's tension is as tight as Bryant's fist.

His eyes narrow. "You're blinded by your emotions and delusions, Mak," he spits out, his words hard. "You have a weakness for broken people, and I'm the best person in your life. You're going to regret this. You'll be sorry."

"I already am." I meet his eyes without flinching, taking a confident step forward. "We're done, and we've been done for a long time. I choose Paul because he is an amazing person who's lived through hell and deserves happiness. I won't stand by while you belittle him or me."

Bryant hisses, "You man-hating bitch. You need—"

"That's enough, Bryant," Jessica's voice cuts through the room like a scalpel. "Mak deserves respect. You aren't the person I thought you were. And being with you seems like it would've been hell. You are sabotaging Mak's career and her happiness. She doesn't need you!"

His face turns purple, and the veins in his forehead throb dangerously. With no one standing by him, he's outnumbered and outmatched at the nursing station.

Jessica holds my hand, and I keep my ground. *I can't believe I was going to marry him.*

"Is there a problem here?" Marianne approaches, flanked by the hospital's CEO and CFO. Her presence and voice command our attention.

Bryant's face pales, but he quickly attempts to regain his composure, brushing invisible lint from his scrubs. "No problem at all—a small personal disagreement."

She turns to me. "Doctor, would you care to share your opinion?"

I exhale, and with Jessica and the staff at my side, I explain, "A patient and I have a prior relationship. He's an incredible army veteran who's overcome the loss of his entire platoon. Bryant, my *ex*-fiance, is angry, jealous and causing a scene. He's been disrespectful to me and the patient. It's inappropriate, and I won't tolerate it."

The nods from Jessica and the rest of the staff serve as a powerful confirmation of their unwavering support for me in this difficult position and defending my queerness and Paul's differences.

The management team exchanged glances before addressing Bryant. Marianne asks, "And what about you, Bryant? Do you have anything to add?"

He shifts uncomfortably, his smile faltering. "It's a misunderstanding. No harm intended."

The atmosphere shifts, and silence envelops the nursing station.

"It's more than a misunderstanding when you lodge a complaint detailing Doctor Makayla's private, personal life to everyone at the hospital. And you shared a patient's personal information with the entire management team. Complaining to Human Resources about a doctor breaching the hospital's rules insinuates you are intending harm. And emailing every management member was a big mistake."

My heart pounds in my chest as I fix my gaze on Marianne, feeling a lump forming in my throat. The air has been sucked out of the room, leaving me drowning in my anxiety. The weight of her words hangs heavily in the air, threatening to shatter everything I've worked so hard for.

Marianne, my Catholic godmother, holds a place of utmost respect. Her unwavering faith and moral compass have helped me to become who I am today. *How can I face her disappointment? How can I bear the thought of being ostracized by someone whose love and acceptance mean the world to me?*

I stare at Marianne, my mouth dry. Jess told me Bryant was complaining, but I cannot believe he did this. He told them *everything.*

"Bryant, we don't fire people based on their sexual orientation or for past relationships with patients," Marianne states firmly.

Jessica glares at Bryant, and I shake my head in disbelief. *Was he hoping to get me fired? Or was he being spiteful for being rejected?*

Marianne continues, "We do, however, take privacy and workplace harassment seriously. Our staff must be professional and compassionate to *each other and our patients.*"

Bryant nods begrudgingly, his jaw still clenched.

Marianne turns to me. "Doctor, I'm sorry you've been dealing with this situation. And Mak, on a personal note, I am here for you and like your coworkers, I stand by you."

Bryant starts, "Seems a little unfair-"

She cuts him off and continues, "Considering your commitment to respectful and compassionate care, we are establishing a hospital committee to promote inclusivity and equality. We'd like to offer you the position of leading this committee."

My surprise must be visible since Jess nudges me. *Instead of being fired, the hospital is promoting me!*

The doctor beside me shakes my hand, and the nurses congratulate me.

"I'm honored and very surprised. Thank you," I respond sincerely.

Marianne nods and turns her attention back to Bryant. "I didn't expect to walk into this, but since we are here. . ." She looks to the other hospital management staff and continues, "Bryant, your actions directly violated our privacy laws and hospital policy. We are terminating your employment, effective immediately."

"You can't fire me!"

Marianne meets his stare. "Patient confidentiality is non-negotiable. And creating a hostile work environment is an automatic termination. Human Resources is expecting you," she says, dismissing him.

With that, Bryant storms away, leaving behind the crowded nursing station and me, a smile on my lips.

Marianne nods to me, and the management team disappears, leaving the nurses' station to return to normal activity.

Co-workers congratulate me on my new position, and I realize I'm more popular than I thought.

"Hey, I'll still see you for dinner tomorrow, right?" Marianne asks.

"Yes, of course," I say and hug her tightly.

She whispers, "You know your mom is proud of you no matter what. She always loved you and I love you, too, Sweetie."

A tear rolls down my cheek, and I nod, not trusting my voice. I'm becoming quite the emotional Psychiatrist.

Also, I'm relieved by not worrying about losing my job, Marianne, and hiding my feelings for Paul. I exhale with a wave of relief washing over me. *Finally, I can explore my new feelings, be myself, and embrace whatever the future holds.*

In that moment of liberation, I see an older couple standing by the door. As if on cue, Paul stands behind them, his gaze fixed on me and eyes wide.

Jessica spots them simultaneously and quickly says, "Sorry folks, I'm getting those discharge papers."

She turns to me and bites her lip, then mouths, *Oh. My. Gawd. I'm so sorry!*

I don't need to be an expert lip reader to understand her since I feel precisely the same way.

How much did they hear?

Chapter 17

Paul

Preparing to leave the hospital, flanked by my parents, with my pop still apologizing for not catching me when I fell, my attention is diverted not by the gusting Alaskan winter outside but by her - *Mak.*

She's standing at the nurses' station, her voice a melody of confidence and assertiveness, tugging at my heartstrings. The scene unfolds like a movie's dramatic climax: the underdog confronts the bully and wins.

I'm stunned witnessing her raw honesty, which makes me want to hug her and give Bryant the knuckle sandwich he deserves. She's brave and unflinching, making my turmoil pale in comparison.

My mom, holding the carnations, looks at my dad with a smile. My pop puts his hand on my shoulder and squeezes as we stand there, a silent trio, while Mak admits to loving me and confronts the man who was once her partner.

My parents remain quiet, and my mom's gaze shifts to me. "Looks like you've got a cheerleader, huh? Better not let this chance slip away."

"Get her number this time," my dad quips, propelling me forward.

Thanks, Pops! The movement makes Mak and my nurse turn, flushing when they spot us.

Jessica approaches, fidgeting and apologizing.

Mak rushes over, and her approach breaks the tense silence after the dramatic scene.

A nervous smile tugs at my lips, and I nod to Mak as she approaches us.

"I'm sorry about that. I'm Mak. It's lovely to meet you," she says, holding her hand to greet my parents.

My mom nods and takes her hand. "Sandy and Ben. We are Paul's parents. We heard all about you, and it's lovely to meet you, too."

My mom's hand doesn't let go of Mak's, and she says, "Doctor Mak, we can't thank you enough for what you've done. We haven't seen Paul this happy in a long time." She pauses and looks at my dad.

"We could have done without the emergency bringing us here, but it's worth it to meet you in person." My dad grins and nods.

"You are a true blessing to our family, and we're grateful," my mom continues, gushing.

"Hey, glad to see you," I say to Mak, biting my lip at my parent's over-the-top greeting.

Mak's flush creeps down her cheeks to color her neck as she looks at me. She turns to my mom. "Thank you for your kind words. It's an honor to help Paul and meet you." Mak moves her other hand to extract her hand from my mom.

Instead, Mak's hands circle my mom's hands, and she squeezes them, adding, "I am so sorry if you witnessed that inappropriate scene. Paul is an incredible person, and he deserves respect."

My mom looks at Mak sideways and holds her hands, squeezing back. "I wanted to extend our condolences for your parents. I saw they passed, and they were lovely people. I'm so sorry," my mom adds.

My dad nods.

I fill the uncomfortable silence by pulling Mak's Santa hat from my pocket, which dislodges the Saint George medallion, and it clatters on the hospital ER tiles.

"That medallion was from your father. He was my special friend, and I miss our long talks. We served together." my dad says to Mak as I bend to pick up the medallion.

Mak's eyes widen, and her plump lips part, a blend of surprise and disbelief in her eyes. Her hand touches the St. Michael medallion on her throat, under her scrubs.

My parents knew Mak's parents! My dad's war buddy is Mak's dad. What?

"I went to the cabin hoping to find his medallion. I remember it pressed against my cheek when he hugged me tight when I was younger. It was such a part of him and comfort to him and me." Her eyes glaze with a nostalgic, faraway stare, and tears collect in the corners.

My dad says, looking at me, "I gave it to Paul."

I stand, holding the silver chain and medallion. My mom gives me a nod, and I turn to Mak and reach out to hand her the chain.

The tears spill, and she bites her bottom lip, taking the medallion from my hand and holding it to her chest. Then her face softens, and a smile forms when she looks at my dad and then at me.

"Paul, can I really have this?"

Her whispered question is heartbreaking. "*Of course.* It's your father's. It's yours."

"I replaced the chain," my dad says.

I move my hand over hers and then place the necklace over her head so it lays against her chest and her heart.

Mak turns to me and puts her hand back over her St Michael's and St. George's medallions. She removes a chain, holds it in her hand, and looks at me.

I'm uncertain, but I nod as she reaches around my neck to secure the chain around my throat. The weight feels familiar, and I realize she's given me back her dad's medallion and kept hers. The weight is similar to wearing my dog tags again. I smile a thanks to her.

Then, with her gleaming, wet eyes, she explains, "I think Saint George can bring you peace, and my dad would've liked you to have it." Her warm breath tickles my ear and warms my insides.

I take a steadying breath, summoning courage. "Mak, I'd like to ask you for your phone number and a proper date."

Before Mak can answer, Jessica holds her hand, stopping the conversation. "No! Sorry to interrupt, but I need you to sign the discharge paperwork, Paul. We can't have a hospital committee head dating a patient. Let's make you *legally* available."

Mak laughs, and her laughter breaks the seriousness that enveloped us, making a cascade of chuckles escape me.

My mom nudges me, and my pop winks.

"Paperwork first," she says and steps back for Jessica to hand me the forms.

I chuckle as I swiftly sign the papers, and my hand shakes as I give the clipboard back to Jessica.

"Are they proper now?" my mom asks.

"Mom–" I start.

"Has Paul ever been proper?" my dad asks.

I smile at Mak and shake my head. "So, about the date …"

"Yes. Let me give you my number so you don't have to have an emergency to see me," Mak says, her grin infectious and my parents laughing at her joke.

Spontaneous and unexpected applause erupts from the Emergency Department staff, catching me off guard, and my cheeks heat with embarrassment. *We are parent-approved and staff-approved.*

She graciously bows to the applause and jokes, "I'll sign autographs in the breakroom later. Now, go back to work and stop gossiping!"

As the applause subsides, I look at her, and the spark between us warms me. She is gorgeous, even in scrubs.

"I'm looking forward to your call and our date, Paul," she says, pressing her wet lips together, and her warm brown eyes melt me.

"Me too."

My parents laugh. "We all are!" They embrace Mak warmly, and I see tears in my dad's eyes.

"I should have caught Paul so he didn't hit his head," he says again.

"His head is hard, and he needed the excuse to see me," she responds and winks at me.

"How about we go out and warm up the car?" My mom nudges my dad, and they wave as they head into the snowy parking lot.

Without my parents and the hospital staff scattering, Mak and I stand together.

"You know," she whispers with a playful smile, "I still have bacon, bananas, and sourdough bread at the cabin."

I laugh, my heart light and free. “Elvis sandwich date?”

She grabs my hand. “A stupendous idea! I love it but *after* our date. I don’t want to rush you into the commitment of bacon mixed with fruit too soon.”

“But you already have,” I laugh and hug her.

She melts into me. “I know. I’ve ruined you!” she whispers, her warm breath on my neck. “Um, and I still get to enjoy feeling the St. Christopher charm.” She presses her soft breasts further onto me, our tender embrace intensifying as her warmth fills me.

“I’m on to you, Dr. Mak,” I say with a smile, untangling from her arms before this embrace ruins me further.

“I’ll let you walk the patient out,” Jessica calls out, breaking us up, and shoos Mak and me to the door and out into the cold.

Jessica really missed her calling as a waitress-she interrupts at the *worst possible moments.*

Alaska isn’t too unbearably cold when we step outside into the wind and snow. I have her warm hand in mine as we walk, fingers intertwined into the biting weather. The familiar sensation of Mak’s touch makes my heart race in anticipation, the same feeling I had at our first touch.

There’s an unthawing of the last icy layers around my heart.

Did I rescue her, or did she save me?

Epilogue: Mak

"It's here." I turn to Paul, handing him the envelope.

Paul brushes his hands on his flour-dusted apron from making biscuits and gravy for breakfast, his Alaska specialty with reindeer sausage. Since we moved to the cabin last year, his cooking skills have improved. My days are filled with remote hospital board work, online counseling, and organizing outdoor hikes with my patients for PTSD therapy.

"Thanks!" he says, taking the envelope from my hand.

We sit in front of the fire, and he slowly opens the envelope while I hold my breath. The paper emerges, and he unfolds it with a plastic card falling out. He picks up the card, and his eyes fill with emotion, then hands it to me.

It's *Paul Jacob*'s new Alaska driver's license with his updated picture.

I whoop with joy. "It's official—I'm marrying Paul next year!" I give him a big hug, and we laugh together.

Apart from relocating my practice to the Caribou Hills and Paul moving into the cabin with me, the most significant change in our lives has been getting engaged and Paul's determination to be legally recognized as a man before our wedding. He's always known he's Paul, but his battle with depression had hindered him from taking this step. This license is the final confirmation, the acknowledgment of the man I love.

Seventeen months have passed since that fateful Christmas Eve winter when our paths converged. Our love blossomed like the wildflowers adorning the hills. We've grown closer, our hearts joining in the beautiful Caribou Hills.

Paul's resilience and strength warm my heart. He's confronted his demons and found solace in the camaraderie of fellow veterans during the therapeutic forest bathing hikes I manage for the group.

His determination inspires us all, a testament to the strength of the human spirit. Even though he prefers solitude and nature, he still joins me at hospital social functions and the local Caribou Hills Cabin Hoppers parties.

My work has evolved. I continue to run hospital committees, but I've set up my psychology practice from the comfort of our cabin. In the wilds of the Caribou Hills, I've found a unique way to help veterans on their path to healing.

I organize therapy hikes in the summer, and in the winter, we snowshoe. I invite the veterans to immerse themselves in the wilderness, as it played a significant role in my journey to self-acceptance and finding peace.

Surrounded by the tranquility of nature, the tundra becomes a safe space for them to share their stories and confront their trauma. The healing power of the tundra, the moose, and the blisters they get from carrying a rucksack is astounding. I'm honored to guide them on their path to recovery.

Paul hikes with us, and our love deepens with each passing day. Our cabin, once a refuge for our hearts, is now filled with the memories of a love that thrives despite adversity.

As we stand on our cabin's porch, gazing at the vast expanse of the Caribou Hills, gratitude fills my heart. My prayers are filled with gratitude for the love God brought me during a deadly blizzard, for Paul's strength on his healing journey, and for the breathtaking Alaskan wilderness.

Paul turns to me, his eyes shining with love and a hint of mischief. "You know, Mak, I'm so lucky to have you in my life."

I grin, my heart overflowing with love. "And I can't imagine my life without you, Paul. You've warmed my cold feet on the worst winter nights."

Paul laughs. "Is that going to be in your wedding vows? Why won't you wear wool socks? Why must you test our love every night?"

I laugh. "I can't sleep in socks, silly. Besides, you are the one who likes to sleep without any layers between us."

Paul shakes his head and pulls me close. Our lips meet in a tender kiss, sealing our love amidst the beauty of Alaska. The winds whisper their blessings as the Caribou Hills bear witness to our ever-evolving love story.

If you loved Mak & Paul's sapphic adventure, then you'll love Baby and Poppy in *Wilderness Rescue: Winning Love.*

CHECK IT OUT HERE or at HarmonyNoble.com.

Discover the books in the *Wilderness Rescue* series.

CHECK IT OUT HERE.

Keep reading to enjoy the next book.

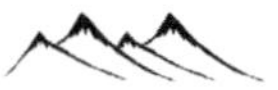

Wilderness Rescue: Winning Love
Chapter 1:

Win·ning

Dictionary – Definitions from Oxford Languages

/ˈwiniNG/

Adjective

1. gaining, resulting in, or relating to victory in a contest or competition. *a winning streak*
    - Similar: victorious, successful, conquering, triumphant, unbeaten, first, top
2. attractive; endearing. *a winning smile*
    - Similar: engaging, persuasive, charming, appealing, sweet, cute, pretty, attractive, lovely, captivating, enchanting, adorbs

/'winiNG/
Noun

1. money won, especially by gambling. *He went to collect his winnings.*
    - Similar: prize(s), money, gains, spoils, booty

Shplop!

My cold, wet bra falls on my face from the makeshift clothing line stretched across the narrow room, and my bunk jumps under me in an off-kilter way.

What in the unbuttered sourdough muffin is going on?!

Groggy and disorientated, my eyes open to darkness, the room tilting and water rushing in. I flail in the dark, panic surging through my veins as I roll, scrambling out of my bunk, and open the hatch into the dark hallway.

Chaos erupts as people rush past, shouting and shoving into the tiny space. My heart pounds, and my mind races as I fight against the crowd in the narrow hallway, trying to get up onto the ship's deck.

It's the Titanic! I'm in a death trap. I will drown stuck inside or die freezing in the arctic waters!

I must escape! My mind relives the movie scene with people falling off the rails into the gray, icy water—*OMG, why do I always default to the worst-case scenario?*

I see her, my Leonardo DiCaprio. She's a whirlwind of color and energy amidst the chaos-*Poppy*. My mind slows to take in the scene of Poppy wearing her comfy, brightly colored workout gear and hiking boots. Her caramel, sun-kissed skin, shiny black hair, and athletic physique make it impossible to mistake her for another crew member. Like me, she's an Alaskan indigenous woman. And she is also my secret summer crush.

"Come on, *Baby!*" Poppy calls out, her voice calm amid the panic. She grabs my hand and pulls me to the emergency exit.

I grasp her, my lifeline, as I stumble along to safety.

"It's Bailey," I whisper breathlessly and tighten my grip, securing my connection to her hand. Unlike Leo's character, dramatically releasing Kate, *I'm not letting go!*

Weeks ago, I got the courage to introduce myself to her, the most gorgeous crew member at the ship's Bon Voyage Mixer. I'm shy and barely talk to other crew members, and no one knew my name to introduce us, so I bravely approached her and introduced myself. But with the loud music, she misheard me and has called me "Baby" ever since.

I meant to correct her, but how she says *Baby* melts my heart, like drinking a hot dark mocha on a cold winter night. Since I never corrected her, and she's socially assertive, she *helpfully* introduced me to the rest of the crew. For weeks, I've been answering to the name *Baby.*

I'm changing my name. That's the obvious, least-embarrassing solution.

Poppy doesn't hear me. She kicks her hiking boot into a cabin door, whooping when it opens with a loud pop. Her vibrant brown eyes sparkle with determination, and her free-spirited laugh is out of place in this dire situation but entirely predictable for her. She propels people to the upper deck.

"Keep moving, Hector!" She shouts back to the dishwasher, whom I've never talked to before, let alone learned his name.

I bite my bottom lip-Correcting my name doesn't matter. Plus, I don't want to slow her-*us*-down, even though I'd like to go back and get my shoes and my phone. We reach the upper deck hatch together as icy water surges into the hallway, and I gasp as the cold water hits my bare legs.

Crack, a sharp noise hangs in the air as Poppy kicks another hatch open. Then, I am weightless for seconds when we plunge off the rails into the frigid waters of Kachemak Bay.

The shock of the cold water steals my breath. I cling to Poppy, who effortlessly treads water and keeps us afloat. Easy for her-she's a triathlete. I know because I'm stalking—I mean, *following*—her on social media, and sometimes I *accidentally* bump into her when she's working out on deck.

Together—*mostly her pulling us through the water*—we fight against the Arctic current, swimming toward the nearby rocky shoreline.

Thank God it's only two hundred meters away! As I tread the frigid water, a shiver races down my spine, back up my spine, and into my skull, causing my teeth to chatter incessantly. The icy ocean seeps through my pajamas and goosebumps my skin, numbing my feet and moving up my legs. My muscles tense in response to the biting cold, and tiny pins and needles dance through my body.

Is it possible to die of hypothermia while swimming to the nearby beach?

I'm still clinging to her with my death grip, and my toes probably have fallen off my feet since I no longer feel them.

I glance at the impressive Grewingk Glacier. We dropped our cruise guest off yesterday, and it's invisible in the dim morning. The tourists marveled at seeing the "real Alaska" and are tucked cozily at the Driftwood Lodge, where we were supposed to pick them up tonight in this bay overlooking Seldovia. The village of Seldovia is cast in a warm golden glow, nestled in the mountains and bordered by glaciers and the icy water I'm swimming in. The picturesque village's beauty starkly contrasts with the mess unfolding in the bay as the crew yells and the ship sinks.

My feet touch the rocks under the water, I gasp for breath, and I stumble with Poppy going the last five meters. *Perhaps I was overreacting a little, comparing this to the Titanic.*

As we reach the rocky shore, Poppy grins at me. "Baby, we made it, and the sun's coming up. Let's count this as our daily workout!" Then she laughs in pure relief, and I respond with a wordless smile.

I'm not dead! And Poppy holds me up as we crawl onto the rocky beach. If she releases me, my rubber legs will *for sure* give out. I also missed another opportunity to correct her.

It's actually Bailey—my enchanting mermaid—but you can call me Babycakes.

I'll tell her the first part when it's not an emergency. The second part, I'm keeping to myself!

As we stand here shivering and soaked, I'm in my sleepwear: a tank top and shorts. She's wearing her soaked heavy layers, a swimsuit, t-shirt, jeans, and hiking boots that didn't seem to slow her down during our swim.

Instead of being out of breath, she's exhilarated, and I can't deny the fluttering in my chest when she looks at me with her endless brown eyes and long raven hair fanned over her chest. Her vibrant spirit radiates warmth and strength despite our current situation.

She stops laughing to help pull up our other crew, crawling up the beach to join us.

"Look, it's the Titanic," a crew member points.

The colossal cruise ship, once a symbol of luxury and Arctic exploration, is listing at a dangerous angle. It defies logic, its form tilting as if the laws of physics are contorting under the weight of the calamity. I expect it to roll, but the ship dips and bobs before sinking into the bay like a killer whale, appearing and disappearing silently.

"That's... our belongings and our home!" My voice is calm, and the others' hysterical laughing evaporates. "How are we supposed to get paid?" Then I realize how selfish I sound and look at my feet, embarrassed. Of course, we lost our belongings, summer employment, and income, but we are alive and on the beach.

Poppy doesn't say anything about my comments. She meets my eyes, and her eyes mirror my disbelief. "Our summer jobs… They're gone, for sure. And there's no way we are getting our stuff.

"Reality punches me in the stomach, and I lean over dry heaving. *Thankfully, my stomach is pre-breakfast empty.* All my dreams of making enough money to fund my grad school tuition vanished just like our ship.

"We can't just stand here." Her voice refocuses me, and she helps me stand up from my failed vomiting. "We need to help. There are still people in the water. They could freeze before help comes."

As much as I admire her courage, swimming to the sinking ship is absurd. We are lucky not to be dead of hypothermia. "Poppy, no! You can't swim back out there. It's too dangerous."

Her eyes look at where the ship disappeared, and she looks through me and says, "I have to do something. I'm a strong swimmer. I can help."

"Are you out of your mind?" I say, my words cracking with panic. *If she swims out there, she's not returning.*

"You'll freeze out there, and what can you do even if you reach people? We need to find someone with a radio to call for help."

Another person, not a crew member, on the beach overhears and says, "There's no signal here. There's never a cell reception in Seldovia. We don't have any towers."

Panic churns in my stomach as the truth hits me—we're stranded, cut off from the world, unable to reach out for help, and stuck on this beach among strangers with only the wet, cold clothing on our backs.

Polly puts her arm around me, and we look back to the water.

"Damn it!" I shake my head.

Poppy isn't alone in wondering what to do now. I notice the movement of locals coming onto the beach to see the activity in the bay.

A person wraps a heavy blanket around my shoulders, and before I can say thank you, the person moves on to hand a blanket to the next shivering crew member.

"Walk up there, and the volunteer firefighters can help you." A man points up the sloped beach, directing everyone to walk up the hill to town for help.

I don't want to swim out to our coworkers, but walking away feels like selfishly abandoning the crew stuck in the water and swimming to shore. We can only stand on the beach and shout for them to keep swimming.

Poppy grins, and her face lights up, pointing to the fishing boats chugging their way to rescue people. "See,

Baby, the whole village is comin' to the rescue! Alaskans are always ready to lend a hand!"

I exhale and rub my hands together for warmth. My shoulders slump, and I bite my lip, kicking at a rock. "What are we supposed to do, then? Just stand here?"

"Don't worry. We'll figure it out!" Poppy puts her arm back over my shoulder, and we huddle on the beach watching.

What should we do about our situation?

Seldovia is an isolated little community that is not connected to the mainland except by boat. I can't drive, fly, or take a train home. I can't leave by a boat ferry with the bay and docks blocked. Worse, I have no money, phone, or family, and my parents don't expect to hear from me for weeks. They won't even realize I need help.

At least I don't need to reason with her not to dive back into the frigid water.

A sudden burst of commotion breaks through the gloom. A distant roar of engines grows steadily louder. A Coast Guard vessel emerges on the horizon, slicing through the bay.

I say, trembling slightly, "Thank goodness, the Coast Guard's here!"

A ripple of excitement courses through the crowd as the vessel draws closer. It's a majestic sight. Her hand finds mine, and we squeeze each other's fingers.

My hands are warm in hers and wrapped in the wool blanket.

The Coast Guard crew springs into action, deploying their rescue boats and reaching the shipwreck survivors still clinging to debris in the frigid water. Their efficiency and determination are astonishing.

We watch in awe as they pull our drenched crew members to safety. It's a moment of triumph and allows us to relax. Thank goodness Poppy won't be diving back into the ocean again.

She must have read my thoughts. "You know the water isn't that cold here. I take a thirty-minute swim in it on my training days."

"But you swim knowing a warm shower and coffee await you. Also, you're amazing," I say. "The rest of us aren't mermaids. We're more like sloths."

She shrugs her agreement, and we watch as the Coast Guard safely rescues the last crew member. A collective sigh washes over the beach, and we share smiles and high-fives. *We may have lost everything, but we've survived.*

Poppy and I smile, moving our fingers to lace together. The warmth of the blankets and coats chase away the beach's chilly winds. The wind doesn't seem too bad, and the cheering around us almost makes me forget that my toes are numb and we're stranded.

Oh. My. God. We are stranded here with no place to stay and no money!

A bystander's grim assessment reaches my ears, "Somebody must've messed up big time with those repairs. That ship went down fast.

"There's a grumbling agreement and relief that we didn't have any guests on board, and there doesn't appear to be any crew missing. The boat's emergency was unexpected, but we followed our training, and everyone made it out.

It's too bad the navigation crew and Captain are on the Coast Guard vessel-I'd like to give them a piece of my mind. *Who sinks a ship in calm waters near a dock?*

The weight of the situation bears down on me, suffocating my happiness at being so close to my crush and being alive.

Another voice jests, "Well, folks, this is Alaska's way of ending the tourist season. Go get coffee at the Visitor's Center or Fire Station. It's on the house!"

"Frank, the coffee is free there, and no one is going to charge them, anyways," a woman, who is probably Frank's wife, says, poking him.

A reluctant chuckle escapes my lips at the absurdity. The irony of the joke hits home—tourists are nowhere in sight, and our summer is over with our summer employment sinking along with the ship.

The other wet crew members wander up the hill into town with the helpful villagers. Poppy and I, still in a state of disbelief, stay behind and sit huddled together near the rocky shoreline, watching the sun rising and the bay filling with boats and strange equipment. The aftermath of the shipwreck leaves an air of uncertainty hanging over us, and sitting together in silence is comforting.

A figure stumbles towards us as if on cue, his uneven gait revealing his inebriated state. The smell of alcohol wafts from him, fouling the salt-laden breeze. He holds his breakfast beer loosely, the contents sloshing as he nears.

"Hey there, ladiesss," he slurs, his gaze shifting between us.

Poppy's arm tenses under my hand, her discomfort palpable. Linking my arm with hers, I send her a reassuring glance. We are together here.

"Hey," I reply cautiously. My voice's hesitancy matches the unsettling feeling in my gut.

The man's gaze lingers on Poppy, his eyes tracing her wet form in a way that makes my skin crawl. "You two are far from home, aren't ya?" he muses.

Her grip on my arm tightens, her instincts aligning with my own. "We're here for work," she replies.

He chuckles. "Work, huh? Well, the bay's gonna be closed until the Coast Guard's finnish, and I've got a boat. I'll take yous back to Homer, no skin off my nose, any."

His proposition and leering casts an ominous shadow over the already scary situation. The hairs on my neck prickle as I exchange a glance with Poppy.

Poppy stands. "No thanks."

"We're okay," I add, my voice steady and my gut churning.

The man steps closer. "Come on now, sweethearts," he slurs. "You don't need to be alone. I can help yous out."

My grip on her arm tightens, and I dust the sand off my legs, leaving. With a forced smile, I nod toward the village. "We appreciate the offer, but we'll stick around here for a while. Enjoy your walk."

As we step away from his lingering gaze, the unease and the cold make me shiver. Poppy and I quickly walk opposite him, away from town and the almost empty beach. His threatening interaction ruins our excitement of being alive, and I'm tense and cold on a deserted beach.

My breath hitches, and my heart clenches, making me taste acid.

We're trapped in the wilderness—a place without rules, where danger lurks.

I link arms with Poppy, and she confidently walks, slowly navigating the unfamiliar wilderness with me since I'm barefoot with numb toes.

As we walk away, the ocean drowns out any sound of the man.

Chapter 2: Poppy's Winning Scheme

Strolling on the rugged shore, we're quiet, lost in our thoughts as the sun rises.

Baby's anxious vibe is weighing her down-even I feel it. She's frowning at the rocky ground instead of savoring the pink and orange reflecting across the ocean. She chews on her lips, hiding her quirky smile.

I *must* lift her spirits. After all, optimism is my specialty, and choosing hope makes every situation bearable. *We are alive, on a beach with a beautiful sunrise—things could be much worse!*

"Poppy, what are we going to do?" Baby asks as we roam on the rugged shore, the morning stretching to afternoon.

I nudge her playfully. "Don't worry, Baby. Everything's gonna work out. Worrying won't change or help us. The sun is out, we have each other, and we'll figure it out."

My reassuring words are to lift her spirits and *mine.* We *are* in a sticky situation, stranded in this picturesque but unfamiliar part of Alaska. Without money or our phones, it's a little different than a usual hiccup when I travel.

The unknown and traveling to new places don't bother me because I'm training to be an elite triathlete. I travel all over to enter competitions, and I'm always in a strange place with no friends or family. Having the ship sink and being stranded is unexpected, and my competitive mind races to figure out how to win.

If only this were a test of strength or endurance, I know I'd be fine. I swim miles in the Arctic Ocean, trail run over mountains, and bike from Alaska to Canada, but our situation is vastly more complicated.

We need somewhere to sleep tonight and something to eat, then a way back home. *I won't even think about our lost jobs and our paychecks.*

"We could ask the locals for help," Baby suggests, her gaze flickering toward a small group of fishermen.

"The locals—like the guy offering us a ride?"

Baby bends down to pick a flat stone and skims it across the water. 1-2-3 skips. "Was it just me, or did he seem a little. . . creepy?"

I chuckle.

"Oh yeah-definitely a *Creeper.* I doubt he even has a boat."

She looks out over the peaceful water. "But what about our summer work? Do you think we are even going to get paid for the summer cruise season now?"

I pick up the perfect flat round stone, toss it, and it skips eight times. Smiling, I pat her back. "We'll figure it out. Maybe we can find odd jobs around town or something. And hey, worst-case scenario, we could always work the *slime line* at the salmon cannery."

She wrinkles her nose at the thought of standing all day, cleaning the guts out of fish. The slime line is the lowest of the low of jobs in Alaska.

"I can't believe you'd even suggest that."

I wink and give her a grin. "Desperate times, my friend. But who knows, maybe we'll get lucky and stumble upon a pile of gold nuggets."

As if the gods heard my unasked prayer, there's a commotion ahead around the bend in the next little bay. A flurry of activity, cameras, and people scurrying around the beach grab our attention.

A surge of curiosity motivates me, and I gently grasp her arm, encouraging her to move closer. Destiny is providing, and I *refuse* to disregard an opportunity placed directly in our path.

"What in the world is happening over there?" Baby asks.

"Let's check it out," I say.

Amidst the whirlwind of activity, no one notices us wandering among the group despite our damp, odd appearance. We blend into the chaotic mix of people too engrossed in their own world to pay us any mind. Half of them are busy admiring their reflections on their phones, applying beauty products, while the others are preoccupied with their high-tech equipment. It's as if we are invisible in this sea of trendy, technology-obsessed individuals.

Dressed in jeans and shrouded in a weathered blanket, I wander into the fashionably dressed crowd.

I wish I could stealthily acquire one of their shiny, brand-new puffer jackets and a sturdy pair of boots for Baby. She needs the extra warmth, and this touristy bunch wouldn't notice the absence of their photo props, the bright, name-brand cold-weather gear. Likely, they'll never wear it again after their obligatory vacation selfies for social media attention.

"I *must* get a selfie with a penguin," a blonde with two-inch manicured nails whines to another blondie, who responds by ignoring her and holding her phone up, trying to get unavailable cell reception.

Penguins are in Antarctica, not Alaska. This group's tour guide needs to educate these tourists seriously.

"When is the Director's ferry dropping him?" a young guy in the group, hunched over cameras, yells to another who is just as young but holding a clipboard, denoting his authority.

Mr. Clipboard, a Californian-cool guy with shades on despite the sun barely peeking through the clouds, scans the horizon and checks his watch. "He should be here any minute, guys. Let's shoot some nice opening shots and background shots. Go ahead and get started.

"The guys exchange uncertain glances and shoulder shrugs as they set up to film the bay.

This group is clueless about the chaos just past their rocky beach; to be fair, they don't have a direct view of the bay around the corner. Even so, if one of them glanced further than the extent of their camera frames, they'd notice the boats rushing into the bay.

"Did you hear that guy?" Baby says, pointing to a huddle of men with expensive equipment filming the panoramic view of the ocean, mountains, and rocky beach.

"I was distracted by the women looking for penguins." I point to the group of stunningly beautiful women shivering, their sun-kissed blonde hair blown by the wind. They huddle together, forming a circle of golden-haired figures with rosy cheeks clad in stylish, albeit impractical, high-end fashion attire. Their designer parkas, heeled boots, and cashmere scarves do little to ward off the breeze.

Baby giggles with me. She says, "I overheard a snippet of conversation. They are filming and it's their first day."

Well, that explains the commotion and the odd assortment of people.

"It's got to be a reality show. But why out here on a remote beach?" I ask aloud.

She shrugs, and we notice a makeshift camp in the woods, complete with cameras, lights, and chairs lined up, like a movie set for some glamorous camping scene.

The film crew left a big rack of tourist winter gear: overly warm skiing puffer jackets, fleece layers, useless Ugg boots, and hats announcing brand names.

It looks like the wardrobe crew left some goodies for us. I'm sure they wouldn't miss a few items.

Who are these filming tourists? I glance at the white-skinned, blonde-haired bunch, shivering in the warm weather.

An Alaskan visit from the Housewives of California? American Idol tryouts in a unique location?

"Should we ask them what they're doing? They look like they need Alaskan guides," she adds thoughtfully.

"We definitely know the area better than them. I spy the breakfast spread. Let's check that out first." I hook Baby's arm, and we meander from the two groups to tables and RVs in the woods behind the beach.

I can't shake the feeling this is an opportunity as we venture closer. Our stomachs rumble, and we enjoy the abandoned table spread with muffins, fruit, and coffee. *I doubt most of these blondies even eat carbs.*

I snag a muffin and pass one to Baby. "Well, look at us, scavengers in the wild. At least we won't starve."

She takes a bite of the blueberry muffin. "Desperate times call for desperate measures," she says, more determined than anxious.

Baby's cute when she gets motivated! I nudge her and give her a wink.

As we nibble on our impromptu meal and sneak on some fleece ski vests, I unfold a paper, reading:

!!!FOR THE DIRECTOR'S EYES ONLY!!!

The Smoking Hot, Arctic Bachelor

**Description: Get ready for the ultimate Alaskan adventure as ten fearless, beautiful bachelorettes battle it out to win the heart of our very own Arctic bachelor, BURLY! Join us as we take you on a wild ride through the untamed wilderness, where love, passion, and survival skills are put to the test. With Alaskan challenges and steamy, passionate romance, this is one ruggedly unique dating show.*

Bachelorette Challenges:

1. *"Iceberg Surfing": Contestants must ride icebergs in frigid waters while attempting to stay balanced. The last one standing wins. Bikinis or formal dresses are preferred for Bachelorettes.*
2. *"Polar Plunge Date": Bachelorettes go on a date in sub-zero temperatures, dressed in skimpy bathing suits, and must take a dip in an ice-cold Arctic ocean*

to win time with the Bachelor.

3. *"Snow Sculpting Showdown": Contestants create intricate snow sculptures using only their hands and essential tools. The most creative sculpture wins.*
4. *"Salmon Wrestling": Bachelorettes will fish, catching and wrestling live salmon with their bare hands in a freezing river alongside grizzly bears fishing.*
5. *"Blizzard Blindfold Challenge": Contestants are blindfolded and dropped during a snowstorm. They must find their way back to camp without any assistance.*
6. *"Extreme Northern Lights Dance": Bachelorettes compete in a dance-off under the Northern Lights, where they incorporate their best Arctic dance moves into their sexy routines.*
7. *"Eskimo Fashion Show": Contestants have to create stylish outfits from materials found in the Arctic, such as wild seal fur and icicles, and then strut their stuff on an icy runway.*
8. *"Avalanche Escape": Bachelorettes are placed in a simulated avalanche scenario and must work together to escape before the "snow" engulfs them.*
9. *"Arctic Cooking Challenge": Contestants must cook a gourmet meal using only ingredients they can scavenge from the wilderness: aprons and chef hats per Costume Designer.*

These challenges will test the Bachelorettes' beauty,

commitment, and adaptability while providing plenty of entertaining, authentic Alaskan moments for the viewers. Adapt challenges to the environment and materials available—winner (s) to be chosen by the Director or Arctic Bachelor, Burly.

Timeline:

Two weeks of heart-pounding Arctic challenges, romantic rendezvous, and unexpected twists. Who will withstand the elements and capture the heart of our Northern Arctic Bachelor?

Winner Payout:

Our lucky lady will win the chance at true love with our Arctic Wilderness Bachelor and walk away with the generous cash prize of $50,000!

(Winner TBA by the Director)!!!EMPHASIZE: THE INTENSE DRAMA, SULTRY ROMANCE, AND UNEXPECTED VICTOR!!!

"Are they *for real*?" she asks, looking over my shoulder. "This is ridiculous!"

I shake my head, trying to talk over my bubbling laugh. "Did you read the *challenges* list? It's like they think Alaska is a big winter wonderland, all year!"

She rolls her eyes and laughs. "Seriously, *iceberg surfing* and *snow sculpting* in the middle of summer? They clearly did no research before coming here."

I can't stop laughing, and she quiets me by pulling the blanket over our heads before we draw attention.

"And don't even get me started on the *Polar Plunge Date.* We just swam in the bay, it's not something I see any of those women doing for fun!" she adds.

I look at the woefully unprepared contestants. Seriously, I can't imagine any of those stylish models fishing, hiking, and *definitely not iceberg surfing!*

I would watch a show that teaches them to ice fish and build a makeshift shelter. It would be hilarious!

"Yep, those poor ladies have no clue what they've gotten into. It's too bad because I could win this against them."

She raises an eyebrow. "You're not seriously considering entering and winning an Arctic reality show, are you?"

I pause. *I wasn't—until she mentioned it.* "Oh, I am. And *we* are entering! We'll use our Alaskan knowledge and teamwork to outshine these other bachelorettes. Plus, it's $50,000! That's a fortune, more than winning first place at an international triathlon. You need this money for grad school and I need it to start my triathlete career. We'll split it."

"You're crazy, Poppy."

I look at her and lift my eyebrow, giving her my most conspiring look with a grin.

She laughs and then looks at the huddle of princesses. Shrugging, she says, "I guess, I can't end summer without my grad school money—I'm in!"

I smile and clap. "Yes! Let's show them what *real* Alaskan women are made of."

We have a plan. Winning this gameshow is *way more* money than we would've made working on the cruise ship.

She smiles, scrunching her nose.

I grab the papers off the table, scribble her name under "contestant," and hand it to her. "That's the spirit! Now, let's fill out these applications and join our competitors."

Before we iron out our plan, the clipboard manager waves at us. "You two, over here!"

We look at each other and nod, walking over to him. He's tired, and a name tag identifies him as Conner, the "Producer."

Conner's eyes flick between us, his gaze lingering on Baby for a moment longer. "You ladies are here for the show, right?"

"Of course!" I say, giving him my dazzling smile.

He smiles back. "Great! I knew you two were our local contestants. Finish your forms so we can head to camp. We are starting without the Director and Host, but at least we have all ten contestants."

I whisper to Baby, "It's time for *full Alaskan mode,* okay?"

Entertaining tourists on the cruise sometimes means stretching the truth about being Alaskan, like how we live in igloos and travel by dog sled. The crew jokes that this is *full Alaskan mode.* Tourists love it, and we get great tips when we tell them about our fictitious wild Alaskan lives.

She nods and flips through the application, which looks more like a dating application than a work form. I scribble, filling in the blanks with my weight and hobbies. I wink at Baby. "Guess who's an iceberg yoga instructor among the whales on Glacier Bay?"

With a giggle and her quirky smile back, she responds, "Really? I took you for an Arctic canoe guide who dreams of settling down on an Alaskan homestead making rose hip jam for your twenty children."

Our laughter catches the attention of Conner. "Glad to hear laughing. The other contestants are complaining about the cold weather."

He's distracted by an Alaskan beaver fur hat on a crew member. "Can we get that hat in faux fur? Fur is so 2000—No fur on the set!"

As we hurriedly finish filling out the sheets, I glance at the women gathering in camp. They're striking, each one more attractive than the last. The realization hits me—we're about to compete against some seriously stunning women.

I look at my filthy clothes. *I hope this Alaskan guy is looking for more than a blonde with boobs.*

Baby's motivated and snatches my sheet, handing it to Conner so we can join the others in front of the yurts.

Walking away, I overhear Conner talking to a crew member. "Every dating reality show needs an ugly girl and an underdog- you know, for the viewers to root for."

Baby hears, too. She frowns and turns to me. "Am I the ugly one or the underdog?"

"Neither! It doesn't matter what he thinks, remember. We'll charm the Alaskan guy, Burly, and the Director to win."

She nods and smiles, her lips free from biting them with worry.

I'm happy her anxiety is gone, and she's back to her bubbly self. She's shy, but underneath, I see the effervescent, intelligent person she is.

I look around at the shivering, unhappy, beauty-pageant women.

"Baby, you're going to be the winner!"

Continue reading Baby and Poppy's heartwarming story in *Wilderness Rescue*: *Winning Love.*
CHECK IT OUT HERE or at HarmonyNoble.com.

Wilderness Rescue Series

Welcome to the breathtaking wilderness of Alaska, where love blooms as wild and beautiful as the northern lights.

Prepare for an exhilarating journey through diverse, LGBTQ+ inclusive romances set against the backdrop of charming small towns and untamed frontier.

Immerse yourself in a series that celebrates Alaskan culture and heartfelt relationships featuring trans, lesbian, bisexual, and two-spirit characters. From gripping rescues to soul-stirring connections, these standalone sapphic tales celebrate strong women navigating love and life with grit and determination in Alaska's rugged beauty.

Explore the standalone sapphic romance stories in the Wilderness Rescue Seriesat HarmonyNoble.com

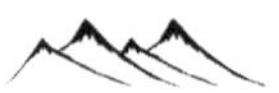

"I loved learning more about Alaska... I also loved when they finally got their happy ending, it was super satisfying."—**Reviewer on Crashing Into Love**

She took the job in Alaska's wilderness to prove herself. Instead, her journey to love is the adventure.

City nurse Riley Thompson has her future perfectly mapped out—until she's stranded in a remote village. The only bright spot? The village elder who saved her life and sees right through her polished outer image.

Mary's wisdom as a Yu'pik elder has guided her people through countless storms, but talking a drunk pilot into landing safety—and saving a beautiful city nurse in the process—might be her greatest test yet.

With Riley's career pulling her back to city life?

Will tradition and personal ambition pull their hearts in opposite directions?

Join us at www.HarmonyNoble.com **to read this love story.**

"Unthaw My Heart" is a thrilling standalone novella to warm your heart and prove love reigns even in deadly conditions."

—Reviewer on Unthaw My Heart

In the harshest of winters, can a Christmas Eve storm turn two broken hearts into something beautiful?

Caught in a Christmas Eve blizzard, Dr. Makayla and Army mechanic Pauline are trapped in a remote Alaskan cabin—facing more than just the freezing cold. In the unforgiving wilderness of Alaska's Caribou Hills, survival is about opening your heart, facing your fears, and finding the strength to trust someone new.

As they navigate icy car crashes, broken promises, and the harsh realities of coming out in a town that feels too small, Paul and Mak discover that love is the one thing that can unthaw even the coldest hearts.

"This is my first Female/female romance I believed and I thought it was very cute and entertaining. The plot line was fresh and unique and I loved the characters."—**Reviewer on Winning Love**

Lights, camera, complication: Two coworkers team up to face off in Alaska's ultimate reality dating show, but when the game is love, who's really keeping score?

Stranded in Seldovia after their cruise jobs sink, Poppy and Baby join the outrageous new hit, The Smoking-Hot, Arctic Bachelor, scheming to win the cash and charm the hunky bachelor.

When prize and love collide, they flip the script, turning the romantic game show into a jaw-dropping celebration of true love.

Join us at www.HarmonyNoble.com **to read this love story.**

"A Riveting Rollercoaster of Love and Life in Alaska!" **—Reviewer on Stormy Hearts**

I steer my ship into the vast sea to lose my past. Instead, I found her. Now I chart a course to search for her lost love... A course that ends in my heartbreak.

In freezing Arctic waters, Maria's world shatters when her husband vanishes overboard, lost to the icy depths of Kachemak Bay. But fearless Alaskan boat captain, Jackie, swoops in to save her from the storm's clutches.

Despite Maria's grief and the town's judgment, their bond deepens, weaving a tale of love against the odds.

As they navigate through the stormy seas of prejudice and their own hidden pasts, they must choose—risk everything for love or let fear tear them apart?

"This novel is an absolute gem! The author skillfully weaves a romance that feels genuine and inclusive. Sterling and Chloe's love story is not just about love but also self-discovery and embracing life's unexpected twists..."—**Reviewer on Scoring Love**

Hockey was her game plan until love changed the rules.

In Fairbanks, where temperatures are at -66°F, a hockey star's perfectly planned life is about to get checked by love.

When hockey hotshot Sterling saves local artist, Chloe, from falling through the ice, neither expects the heat that ignites between them.

Can Sterling trade her player status for Chloe?

Will Chloe risk revealing that the coach tormenting Sterling is her ex-husband?

Join us at www.HarmonyNoble.com **to read this love story.**

"I enjoyed the story a lot. . . some angst, and plenty of comic fun. I enjoy the insights into Alaskan life."—**Reviewer on Flooded Hearts**

In Alaska's wildest kitchen, a chef discovers that the best recipes can't be found in a cook-book when love is on the menu.

When uptight chef Lucy flees her toxic ex and lands in Cooper Landing, Alaska, she has one goal—becoming a Michelin-starred sensation.

Deb—beloved local farmer and keeper of indigenous traditions—believes any disaster can be fixed with wisdom and a community feast.

A flash flood threatens their tiny town, throwing these opposites together. Lucy—who doesn't do chaos or feelings—finds herself knee-deep in a rescue.
As her orderly life unravels, could messy, wholehearted Deb be exactly what she needs?

"A captivating journey of love and self-discovery that will stay with you long after you've turned the last page."

Sometimes the steepest mountains lead to the sweetest collisions-a story of skiing, healing, and love.

Get ready to race down the ski slopes where two paths cross on a wild ride of love and self-discovery.

Caitlyn, affectionately known as Cat, must overcome her inner turmoil and grumpiness to reclaim her belief in herself to find love.

Peekaboo is a dedicated ski instructor with an infectious zest for life that inspires others with disabilities to embrace joy and adventure. Yet, behind her smile is a heart yearning for more.

Torn between loyalty to her devoted partner and a longing for fiery passion, will Peekaboo choose love?

Join us at www.HarmonyNoble.com **to read this love story.**

"If you love opposites-attract romances that make your heart race, this is your next favorite book." **—Reviewer on Tides of Love**

Some days change your life forever. This is one of them.

Serena lives for adventure, but when a storm sweeps her into a dangerous rip tide off, she ends up stranded on a rocky outcropping, face-to-face with a cute, but unimpressed local.

Bree, a self-proclaimed Alaskan loner, wants nothing to do with the thrill-seeking surfer. But when the rising tide traps them, they'll have to rely on each other to survive.

What starts as a fight for survival turns into something much more—one storm, one day, and an undeniable connection that neither of them saw coming.

"...If you are a fan of insta-love, this novella will be right up your alley. It is a cozy, sweet romance, with an exciting backdrop of the Alaskan Iditarod." **—Reviewer on Iditarod Love**

Love, survival, and the untamed Alaskan wilderness collide in the race of a lifetime.

Brace yourself for a thrilling journey on snow-swept trails of interior Alaska.

Brynn Dawson has ice in her veins and one goal—winning the Iditarod with her legendary dogsled team. But nothing prepares her for Morgan, an upbeat race volunteer with a knack for getting under her skin.

When disaster strikes during the start of the race on the crowded streets of Anchorage, their worlds collide in a daring rescue that ignites something neither of them saw coming.

Coming Next

AURORA'S WILDERNESS LOVE: HOT GIRLS SUMMER LOVE

Where the odds are good, but the goods are odd—welcome to Alaska, where finding love is wilder than the wilderness.

Aurora knows two things for certain: dating in Alaska is a contact sport, and survival isn't just about navigating frozen tundra—it's about navigating the heart. Broke, desperate, and one dating disaster away from giving up, she's determined to rewrite her story, one hilarious misstep at a time.

With more men than women in this last-frontier dating landscape, Aurora is about to discover that finding herself might be the greatest adventure of all. Armed with nothing but her wits, a killer sense of humor, and an uncanny ability to turn romantic catastrophes into comedic gold, she's ready to prove that sometimes love finds you when you least expect it—and usually when you look absolutely ridiculous.

Get ready for a heartwarming Alaskan rom-com where hunting for love is the ultimate wilderness sport, and Aurora is determined to bag her happily ever after.

In Alaska, the ice is cold, but the workplace tension is scorching

Other Titles by MELODY BEST
& HARMONY NOBLE
For the most up-to-date list visit
www.HarmonyNoble.com

Aurora's Wilderness Love:

Hot Girl Summer Love
Just a Little Fall Crush
Christmas Cruise Mistake

Wilderness Rescue Sapphic Romance Series:

Crashing Into Love
Unthaw My Heart
Winning Love
Stormy Hearts
Scoring Love
Flooded Hearts
Healing Hearts
Tides of Love
Iditarod Love
Frozen Hearts

Coffeehouse Romance Series:

Love, Joy & Lattes (Joy's Story)

Test Driving a Millionaire (Tara's Story)

Shattering Crystal a Bully Romance (Crystal's Story)

Choosing Love, Namaste (Meaghan's Story)

The Wrong Bride for Christmas (Monica's Story)

Coffeehouse Romance Short Stories:

Joy's 4th of July Holidate

Tara's Valentine Holidate

Crystal's Easter Holidate

Meaghan's New Year Holidate

Monica's Halloween Holidate

My Accidental Christmas Fiancé

Joy's Coffeehouse Romance

Snag the latest swoon-worthy reads and stay tuned for upcoming stories at www.HarmonyNoble.com.

Experience the King of Flavors with Our Elvis-Inspired Sandwich: Peanut Butter, Honey, Banana, & Bacon – a Rock 'n' Roll Delight for Your Mouth!

INGREDIENTS

- 4 MEDIUM SLICES OF SOURDOUGH **BREAD**
- 4-6 SLICES OF **AMERICAN BACON**
- 4 TBSP **PEANUT BUTTER**
- 2 **BANANAS**, SLICED INTO SMALL CHUNKS
- HONEY DRIZZLE

DIRECTIONS

1. Add bacon to a large non-stick pan & cook over medium heat until crispy. Remove bacon, leaving the fat in the pan.
2. Lightly butter one side of each slice of bread. Flip them over so they're butter-side-down. Spread peanut butter over all four slices, then top two of them with banana then bacon. Drizzle honey over the bananas . Put sandwiches together with butter facing outside.
3. Place sandwiches in pan. Fry each sides over medium heat until golden, peanut butter may start oozing.
4. Cut in halves & serve up this sweet, savory, gooey delight.
5. Enjoy!

About Author -
Melody Best & Harmony Noble

Meet the unstoppable twins from the rugged wilds of Alaska, the writing duo, Harmony & Melody. Fueled by endless lattes, their character-driven stories brim with authenticity, humor, and heart—featuring Alaskan grit, journeys of self-discovery, and swoon-worthy happily-ever-afters.

When they're not crafting adventure romances, these twins can be found hiking trails with breathtaking views, enjoying charming coffee shops, or exploring new worldwide destinations together.

Join the e-newsletter for exclusive content and give-aways at website: https://harmonynoble.com

Email: TrueLoveWriters@gmail.com
Instagram/Facebook/TikTok: @truelovewriters

www.ingramcontent.com/pod-product-compliance
Lightning Source LLC
La Vergne TN
LVHW010657110826
845149LV00014B/3127